"You can't just call after all of these years with a possible new lead and not expect me to run back here, ready to help. I'm part of this."

A boom of thunder wrapped in rain put Lily further on edge.

"I said I thought I found a potential lead and that I'd call the moment I knew something else," she countered. "I told you I'd keep you updated."

Lily's words were professional, analytical.

It was the only way she could handle seeing Ant in person.

Flip the emotional switch was her mantra when it came to work.

When it came to what happened in the woods when they were teens?

She couldn't *feel* or she'd be overwhelmed.

Ant didn't seem to be struggling in the holding-back department. His brows drew in. and pointed a finger at her.

"I may not have a ba— the department, but sister. My respon— new about this case— now. So I'm here. And I'm not— you can prove to me that the lead— end. I'll be back in the morning, and every morning, until then."

COLD CASE CAPTIVE

TYLER ANNE SNELL

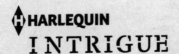

This book is for Regan. Your daily support during this book meant the absolute world. Without your ear, without your encouragement, Lily and Ant would probably still be sleuthing somewhere in my head. You're the absolute best.

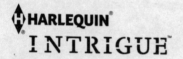

ISBN-13: 978-1-335-48965-4

Recycling programs for this product may not exist in your area.

Cold Case Captive

Copyright © 2022 by Tyler Anne Snell

For questions and comments about the quality of this book, please contact us at CustomerService@Harlequin.com.

Harlequin Enterprises ULC
22 Adelaide St. West, 41st Floor
Toronto, Ontario M5H 4E3, Canada
www.Harlequin.com

Printed in U.S.A.

Tyler Anne Snell genuinely loves all genres of the written word. However, she's realized that she loves books filled with sexual tension and mysteries a little more than the rest. Her stories have a good dose of both. Tyler lives in Alabama with her same-named husband and their mini "lions." When she isn't reading or writing, she's playing video games and working on her blog, *Almost There*. To follow her shenanigans, visit tylerannesnell.com.

Books by Tyler Anne Snell

Harlequin Intrigue

The Saving Kelby Creek Series

Uncovering Small Town Secrets
Searching for Evidence
Surviving the Truth
Accidental Amnesia
Cold Case Captive

Winding Road Redemption

Reining in Trouble
Credible Alibi
Identical Threat
Last Stand Sheriff

Manhunt
Toxin Alert

CAST OF CHARACTERS

Lilian Howard—After making an impossible choice as a teenager to save a boy's life, this detective is back in Kelby Creek years later as part of the cold case task force. It isn't until a current case ties back to her worst nightmare that Lily realizes she might need the boy she saved as kids to save her this time.

Anthony "Ant" Perez—Losing his sister to an abduction he couldn't stop, this older brother has spent the years since with no direction but the past. So when the woman he's never stopped thinking about calls him with a lead, he's on her doorstep the same day. And when he realizes the danger she's in, he vows to stay.

Ida Perez—Abducted in front of her brother and Lily, she's been missing for fourteen years.

Kenneth Gray—Head of the cold case task force, this detective helps Lily navigate the line between the past and the present.

Sheriff Blake Bennet—Newly elected to the Dawn County Sheriff's Department, she's fiercely protective of her people.

Arturo Hanson—A man with unknown motives and ties, he brings on the first wave of danger for Lily and Ant.

Prologue

"The truth is, everyone has forgotten the truth. One of them, at least."

Lillian Howard had her accordion folder tucked beneath one arm, her hair wrapped up in a tight bun, and a tone that was equal parts respectful and professorial.

Detective Kenneth Gray, decidedly not a student but head of the department's cold case task force, kept her stare with rapt attention. He had, as a matter of fact, been the one who had originally called her in for an interview. They'd already gotten the technical parts out of the way—her resume of working at a sheriff's department in north Alabama after deciding to forgo a career at the FBI, even though he didn't ask why she denied the job and she didn't offer an explanation—and now they had arrived at the chitchat part. The human element.

The *let's see if you'll fit in here* back-and-forth.

Too bad for her that she rarely abided by normal social conventions.

Even when she really wanted the job.

All Kenneth had had to do was open the floor for some polite conversation after leaving the meeting room and going to his office and she'd bowled into it, trying her best to get a strike.

"And what truth is that?" he asked.

Lily was glad to hear that there was no condescension in his words. Her former colleagues had been less than welcoming. It probably hadn't helped matters that she was on the younger side and had an intense love for order, which had gotten her labeled as a control freak. Though she preferred "type A" instead.

Then there was her memory. It stretched as long as it did far.

Lily finally took her seat across the desk from him. She put the accordion folder on her lap and recited a speech she'd given countless times in her much younger years.

The ball was now gliding down the alley.

"That Annie McHale wasn't the first young girl to go missing in Kelby Creek."

She unwrapped the worn string from around the folder's latch but decided not to open it yet. The folder was filled with papers, pictures and her own notes. Some were newer, some were in slightly smudged pen written by a seventeen-year-old Lily.

"Annie McHale was taken five years ago," she continued. "Ida Perez was taken fourteen years ago at the age of sixteen."

Lily fought the urge to adjust how she was sitting in the chair. She knew she was rigid—she often became that way when she was focused—but this time it was from the memory of the cold that day. The lingering but still-powerful effect of seeing the police lights strobe against the trees, feeling the chill of the creek against her soaked skin, and knowing by the look on the adults' faces that there would probably be no happy ending.

It was a hard pull to the past that Lily had tried to distance herself from as the years had gone by.

Yet Kelby Creek, Alabama's past had proven to be extremely persuasive.

That's why she was here.

That's why she'd agreed to come back.

That's why she hoped Detective Gray listened.

For now, at least, he didn't stop her. So she gave him the facts.

Concise, emotionless facts.

"Ida Perez was outside talking with her brother, Anthony, when, after he looked away for a second, she disappeared. Shortly after he realized she was gone, a teenaged neighbor heard Ida scream a few houses down. Together they followed the sound through the back end of the neighborhood until they made it to the beginning of the woods. The neighbor managed to see that Ida was with an adult male but it had started to get dark and rain. They couldn't make anything else out." Lily fought the urge to move again. She reached deep inside herself and threw every switch that controlled her emotions to Off. "Ida and her captor went deeper into the woods after that. The neighbor and her brother followed until they got to the creek, where the man attacked Anthony. The kidnapper knocked him unconscious with a rock from the creek bed and then dragged him into the water. It forced the neighbor to make a decision. Drag him out and save him, or chase after Ida.

The neighbor chose to save Anthony. Ida and the man were never seen again."

There.

Concise.

Factual.

Detective Gray leaned forward. He ran a hand across his jaw and nodded.

"It's not lost on me the connection between Annie and Ida. Just like it's not lost on me that this town seems to have glazed over Ida's disappearance and not Annie's."

Lily pushed her shoulders back, not that they weren't already in perfect posture.

"Before what happened to Annie made national news, this entire town dropped everything to try and find her," she reminded him. "It shouldn't matter if you come from a rich family or not. That's what you're supposed to do when a child is taken or goes missing. This town failed Ida Perez."

She hadn't meant to sound as bitter as she had.

Lily reeled herself back in so it wouldn't happen again.

Detective Gray simply nodded one more time.

"Well, as you know, a lot of things were mishandled from a lot of different directions in the past. Closed cases, ongoing investigations, evidence logs, false statements, intimidation… It's why this department *now* is fighting so hard to make sure that never happens again. And it's why the cold case task force was formed."

"To make sure old cases were properly handled," she

said, quoting him from the press release almost a year before when the unit was announced.

He nodded.

"It's a job we—and I—take very seriously. Just like the hiring of detectives to the task force." He threaded his fingers together and looked thoughtful. "Our job can be hard, can be difficult, and we can find answers that we don't want. Hell, most of the time we're looking for broken needles in a soggy haystack and then *if* we find them, we're returning them to still-broken families."

"But finding answers can bring closure," she interrupted.

Detective Gray was solemn.

"It can bring closure," he agreed. "And that's the best thing some people can hope to get."

He didn't mention his personal experiences in the matter, even though everyone in Kelby Creek knew about his journey to find answers and justice after his first wife was murdered and her case left cold for years.

"The drive and the desire to find that for families, for loved ones, and to seek justice and a sense of peace for the victims, is what I want the most in the people on this team," he continued. "I *need* intelligent, compassionate and driven detectives, especially since there's still a lot of people who are against the department. Most notably anyone in this department poking around the past."

It was Lily's turn to nod.

"I agree," she finally said when it was clear Detective Gray was waiting for a response. "It's the only thing I've ever been interested in doing. Finding answers. Trying to bring closure."

"It also helps to have a personal connection for this kind of job," he mused. "It's not needed for everyone but it certainly helps those who have it. And I'm guessing that you have one you're trying to sidestep saying. To Ida Perez's case. Can I ask what that connection is?"

Lily turned tight-lipped.

She knew this part was coming, yet it still felt uncomfortable to answer.

She took a moment, something she didn't often do.

Then her voice came out with more emotion than she realized it would.

"I was the neighbor," she said. "I saved Ida Perez's brother from the creek and I'm the last person who saw her alive."

Chapter One

Anthony Perez was staring at the scar next to his hairline while he waited for a call. He ran his finger along the small line and marveled again at how something so thin could be all that was left of so much damage.

Like a drop of water sitting on the ground after a flood destroyed the world around it.

It didn't seem like much to the people who were looking at the puddle but hadn't been around for the flood.

Ant tapped the skin for good measure and then ran his hands back through his black hair. It caused some to cascade over his forehead and hide the scar.

Maybe that's why his hair was a bit longer than seemed appropriate for a thirty-year-old man trying his damnedest to lead a straitlaced, simple life.

Or maybe he knew it had an effect on most women and kept it that way.

His last date had called his hairstyle "yummy."

She'd also spoken in hashtags and asked if he'd been in a fraternity in college.

Ant wasn't knocking a woman who spoke her mind,

or in hashtags, but he had to admit he wasn't a fan of how much *she* wasn't a fan of him saying no to the fraternity question.

And a double no to college in general.

He hadn't had the time for college. He'd barely had the time for high school and the only reason he'd passed that was thanks to a girl who probably had never even said the word "yummy."

Ant checked his reflection one more time before deciding to head back out to the mechanic's floor.

He was one of five who worked at Slaggerman's Auto on the corner of Kinderman and 5th. Despite not being thrilled about living in Justice, North Carolina, he didn't mind the shop. It was work he knew how to do and work that kept him away from others. Mostly.

With one look toward the open garage doors, Ant knew one of the rare interactions he was about to have with their head mechanic, Martin, wasn't going to be a good one.

"Hey, Ant, I just got a call from Tonya out at Fortner and *she* had some interesting things to say about your work." Martin huffed his way through his words all the way to where Ant was standing. Then he took an inadvertent step back. Martin might have been who Ant answered to but that didn't change the blaring fact that Ant was a good foot taller than him. That and Martin was built like a twig while Ant never skipped a workout on his makeshift home gym back at his apartment.

"What did Tonya *out at Fortner* say about my work?" Ant slid back, dipping heavily into sarcasm where he shouldn't have.

Martin didn't seem to appreciate the tone. His face became red as he answered.

"She said not only did you *not* charge her the right amount for her brand-new transmission but you didn't charge her *at all* for her tire rotation and oil change." He put his hands on his hips. The power move still didn't match up to Ant's natural stance. "Is that true? Are you giving away work for free? You do know this isn't a charity, right?"

Ant sighed. Not at all respectful. Then again, he hadn't liked Martin from the first day.

"Tonya is in her seventies, a widow and, according to her ungrateful grandkid who came in with her, she's going to a home in the next year or two," Ant said. "She's also one of Slaggerman's most loyal customers. She's been coming here for almost twenty years. So I did the transmission work fast and cut down on the price because of it. The cost of the oil change and tire rotation I took out of my paycheck. You can check with your wife. She's the one who approved it."

Martin went from a shade of crimson to the color of a stop sign.

"If Tonya is one of our most loyal customers then it should stand to reason she's not going to complain about full price," Martin bit out. "Like you said yourself, she's been paying it for twenty years."

Ant looked down his nose at the smaller man. It was time he crossed his arms over his chest. Martin eyed the move with visible hesitancy.

Now they were at a crossroads. Ant knew this song and dance as well as he knew the first thing he was doing when he got home was putting on his jogging shorts and going right back out to run through his frustration. He'd been here before, with other jobs. With other men like Martin. He could de-escalate, sure, and say what Martin wanted to hear. Keep his job and come back the next day pretending everything was square.

Or he could say exactly what was on his mind and be back in his apartment before lunch, another job search in his future.

Ant might not have gone to college but he was educated enough to understand that everyone followed a pattern.

His was giving lip to people who deserved to receive it.

"I assumed we don't reward our customers' loyalty by taking a leak all over them for twenty years straight." Ant shrugged. "But I guess that's just me."

Martin opened his mouth, shut it, and then opened it again.

Ant imagined if they were in a cartoon, smoke would be coming out of Martin's ears by this point. Instead the other man finally let all of his anger come out in a string of expletives.

Ant didn't pay much mind to it. He'd been cussed out of a job before. In fact, he had a bit of a track record. Some people had Employee of the Month awards. Ant collected You're Fired tirades. So he decided to tune out the angry Martin.

It was how he picked up that his phone was vibrating in his pocket so quickly.

"You know what, I'm going to take this," he interrupted Martin. "But how about I clean out my locker when I'm done and then we can call it a day?"

Ant didn't wait for an answer and walked outside, pulling out his phone as he went.

He might have played it cool to the small man behind him but he couldn't deny that cool turned into a shake-up in his stomach at the caller ID that was across his screen.

Ant cleared his throat and answered.

"Perez."

There was audible movement on the other side of the phone but the voice was crystal clear over it.

"Hi, Ant, it's Lillian. Lily. I'm assuming you got my voice mail last night?"

Ant nodded then felt foolish since she couldn't actually see him.

"Yeah, uh, I mean, yes, I got it," he answered. "I had a long day so I crashed early. Sorry I missed your call."

"That's fine. I was—" More movement. "Sorry, I'm going through some boxes. Um, yeah, I shouldn't have called so late."

There was a pause between them.

Ant opened his mouth and then closed it again. He bounced from one foot to the other.

Lily broke the small silence.

"The reason I called is— Wait, are you in the middle of anything?"

That he could answer quickly. In the background he could still hear Martin raving.

"Not anymore."

"Okay. Well, good, I guess." A sigh, so deep and

genuine, came across the airwaves. It was a sound that Ant hadn't heard in a long, long time. Whatever Lily had called about she was about to bottom-line it. Ant prepared himself the best he could.

Which wasn't enough.

"The reason I called was because I think I might have found something," she said, her voice flat but firm.

His heartbeat sped up.

"You found something?"

They both knew what she was talking about but Lily spelled it out for him.

"Ida's case," she clarified. "Anthony, I think I found a new lead."

Chapter Two

Lily slipped the phone into her jacket pocket and stepped out into the rain. Her detective's badge swung against her chest at the movement. Her heartbeat was on a downward slope. She couldn't believe she'd called him. Yet she hadn't hesitated. Just like she didn't hesitate now.

Lily stilled her badge with one hand and waved an acknowledgment to the interim sheriff, Blake Bennet. Her long red hair was braided down her back, tight and unmoving. She'd been on the job two months longer than Lily had but had adjusted quickly, despite being from the city. Now she went back to eyeing the deep hole dug into the dark, wet dirt of the woods.

"It's a hole," Sheriff Bennet said in greeting.

Her Southern twang was deep but steady. She'd spent her thirty-four years between north Florida, east Georgia and south Alabama and could make a two-syllable word into five real quick. Lily had grown up in Kelby Creek and done a stint a little up north but had shaken the Southern accent.

Most of the time, at least. When she let out any foul

language there was always a curve and syrupy swoop
to it.

The sheriff motioned to where the dirt should have
been flat and covered in grass and underbrush. Instead
there was, true as she said it, a hole. Deep and narrow.
Maybe six feet down, give or take.

Lily traced the space with her eyes.

"Yep. That's a hole, all right."

There was nothing in it.

Sheriff Bennet laughed.

"Not the call you were expecting while you were
knee-deep in files, huh?"

The rain slacked off a little. Lily shrugged into her
jacket.

"Not exactly. Though not the first time I've been
called to look at a hole in the ground. I'm just excited
that there's no one in it."

Lily wasn't kidding. Her last job had put her in the
position to find a man buried in a ditch, killed by his
brother. She'd also had the misfortune of being the detective on call who'd interrupted a man trying to ac-
tively bury a poor woman who'd simply been in the
wrong place at the wrong time. Lily still had nightmares
about that hole. She also still had the scar from the man
when she'd fought him into custody.

Sheriff Bennet took a deep drink of her coffee. Her
demeanor changed to no-nonsense quickly after.

"I know you're cold case task force so I thought I'd
make sure this isn't any kind of—I don't know—Kelby
Creek thing that, as an outsider, I wouldn't get." She
motioned to the woods around them. "My only other

thought was that it might be a hunter's trap. A poorly and incorrectly made hunter's trap."

Lily crouched down and inspected the edges of the hole. The weather had done a number on the dirt but she bet the hole was made with a shovel, not a human hand or animal paw. Not machinery, either. There were no tire tracks leading up to the spot from the dirt road behind them.

"If this is a hunter's trap, I'd agree it's a bad one," Lily decided after a moment. She rubbed her hands along her denim-clad thighs. "It's not far enough into the woods to be useful, never mind how deep and narrow it is."

"Any cold cases with something similar I should know about?"

Lily didn't have a photographic memory but she was damned good at remembering the details when it came to her work. To the men and women who'd been reduced to files on her desk through no fault of their own. It was the least she could do to sit up and pay attention when their stories were in her hands.

"There's nothing in the cold cases I've seen that deals with dug-out holes," Lily answered. "The only one that I've read that even has a mention of a hole was Jessica Tamblin's attack about seven years ago."

The sheriff's eyebrow went up at that. She'd made it clear to Lily that the cold case task force was under the supervision of Detective Gray and, unless it was pertinent to current cases, she was staying out of it. Not her circus, not her monkeys. A refreshing stance given that the cold case task force had been started because of rampant corruption among the higher-ups years ago.

Lily was glad for the extra space to go through the cases in her own way. It was something Detective Gray respected as well. She only gave him updates at their weekly morning meetings. Then she'd go back to her desk and dig in. She liked working solo, after all. A sentiment not shared by her coworker and desk mate, Detective Kathryn Juliet.

She was a chatterbox compared to Lily's relative quiet.

"Jessica Tamblin was floating the creek with some friends and lost her necklace. She went back the next day to look for it and found a man named Albert Johnson shooting up instead. He didn't appreciate the interruption and tried to attack her. She ran but didn't get far after stumbling across a hole. It was only mentioned in the report because the responding deputy tripped over it too and twisted his ankle pretty good."

The two women gazed down as the rain pitter-pattered off their jackets. It was light and had been part of a consistent rain that Kelby Creek had been entertaining for almost two weeks straight. It didn't bother Lily but made her dog, Cook, very grumpy.

"So maybe this is just a hole, then," Sheriff Bennet said. "Not some kind of serial killer's MO."

That got a snort from Lily.

"Of all the issues Kelby Creek has had, serial killers have thankfully not been a part of them."

The sheriff shook her head.

"You better knock on wood with that one. The second we rule something out, there's a good chance in the next second we'll be proven wrong."

Sheriff Bennet took a long pull of her coffee and then stretched.

"Either way I'm going to have someone come out and check on this thing in a few hours," she continued. "If only to satisfy the man who called it in. He was a bucket and a half of anxiety over it. He even made Deputy Park nervous."

The Flood, a nickname for the town-wide corruption investigation that followed Annie McHale's kidnapping, may have happened five years ago, but that didn't stop Kelby Creek as a whole from being anxious. It was as if the entire town had an itchy trigger finger. They could spend their whole lives holding that gun and never use it but, still, it was in their hands ready the second they were scared enough.

Lily didn't blame anyone. How could she after what happened?

Sheriff Bennet waited as Lily took notes, snapped a few pictures on her phone for good measure, before both walked back to the sheriff's truck. She hopped in and rolled down the window. The rain started to hit the black interior as she spoke.

"First night of the fair is tomorrow. I'm not sure what Gray told you but the department is setting up a booth along the thoroughfare. We're parking one of the deputy cruisers there so kids and curious adults alike can crawl through or take pictures with it. The fire department's doing the same. Since you're Cold Case I'm not going to ask you to go but it would be nice if you stopped by.

Especially since this'll be the first time in a long while that the fair is actually back around here."

Lily had already known her answer before the sheriff had stopped speaking. Still she tried to look thoughtful before saying no.

"I've got a lot of work to do, but don't worry. I'm sure the rest of the department will have enough fun for me."

Sheriff Bennet snorted but she didn't try to dissuade her.

"Let us know if you change your mind." The sheriff started to roll up her window but paused. Her brow was creased in question. "What happened with Jessica Tamblin?"

Lily didn't pretend to ponder this question.

"She ended up making it to the creek and a fisherman who was nearby. Her attacker ran and was caught at his home later that night. Jessica, if I'm not mistaken, lives in Kipsy now. She has a kid and two dogs. Seems happy."

Sheriff Bennet nodded.

"It's nice to hear the wins sometimes."

Lily kept her mouth shut. When the headlights had disappeared past the trees, she went back to the hole.

It was nice to hear the wins.

It was impossible to forget the losses.

Her gaze lifted against the rain to the woods around her.

The weight of her phone in her pocket felt like it was pulling down her entire body.

She would never admit it but sometimes in the quiet

of rain and in the kiss of darkness, Lily would see her there.

Arms outstretched, fingers trying to grasp anything—everything. Mouth open but only a strangled sound escaping around gasps for breath. The rain water between the tips of her fingers and the pounding of Lily's heart terrifyingly loud.

The boy drowning beneath its surface punctuating a life-altering choice.

Anthony or Ida?

The rain hitting the leaves of the trees around her back then quieted into the soft rain against Lily now.

She stared into the woods a little longer.

She heard the coughing in her mind. The man, coughing. Now she hoped it would be enough.

Enough to finally get some answers.

Enough to finally find him.

Lily didn't stare into the woods any longer.

She looked down at the hole, trying to dig herself out of the past.

Then she left.

A GREAT EXODUS had taken place during and after The Flood. When Lily came back to town a few months ago she had half expected Kelby Creek to be a partial ghost town. She'd been surprised to see that it was growing, and had been during her absence. She drove away from the sheriff's department that afternoon and headed toward the only bar in town, Rosewater Inn. Once a failing motel, it had been remodeled and expanded. Its parking lot was always full after her shift and tonight she counted fifteen cars in the parking lot as she stopped at a nearby light.

Depending on who rode with whom that was fifteen or so patrons inside.

Fifteen people Lily could connect with, talk to, become friends with.

Fifteen or more chances to expand a social group that no longer existed.

Fifteen people to question.

Fifteen people to wonder about.

Fifteen people to tell her they didn't remember Ida Perez.

Lily's foot pressed down on the gas the second the light went green. She took the street behind Rosewater and followed it to the far corner of Holly Grove. She hadn't been picky when house hunting but couldn't deny she liked the seclusion that being at the end of the last street in the neighborhood gave her. No one came her way unless they had an invitation. Or just needed to turn their car around.

The property also had a bigger yard, something her shiny black three-year-old Labrador, Cook, seemed to appreciate.

What he didn't appreciate was more rain.

Cook met Lily with a frenzy of tail wagging, tongue licking, and runs between her and the back door as soon as she was inside the two-story house.

"Since we have a dog door and you're more than proficient in using it, I'm going to assume you've already discovered it's still raining," she told him, taking care to scan him for any mud. Thankfully, Cook rarely dug, which helped keep the mud and dirt to hardwood floor and tile ratio at an acceptable level. If the rain got any harder, and kept on for two more weeks, then even Cook's good behavior wouldn't help.

Lily opened the baby gate she had latched at the bottom of the staircase, letting him know he was safe to go between floors. It was enough to make him forget all about going outside. He bounded up the stairs, yipping in excitement as he went.

"You'd think you don't sleep up there every single night by the way you fuss when I get home."

Cook gave her a well-timed bark. She shook her head and laughed.

Lily made her one-person dinner from a box and ate it on the couch with the TV on. *House Hunters* showed a family trying to find an old Colonial in Washington. She would have chosen the third house since it was closest to the wife's work but the family ended up going with the first home, something bigger so they could add onto their family in the coming years.

Lily twisted her fork around her "healthy" vegan pasta and thought about the two bedrooms upstairs. One was the master suite. The other was an office. She couldn't imagine it any other way.

It worked for her.

Her job wasn't just a job after all.

Lily finished her food and was debating going up to that same office when Cook jumped up from his spot on the floor next to her feet. He was gentle but flipped to defensive on a dime when it came to guarding Lily and their home. He ran to the door, emitting a low growl, before Lily even heard the doorbell.

"Cook, calm," she said, dipping her voice down. Lily had her service weapon in hand by the time a knock followed the first ring. She looked into the peephole, already running through a list of people it could be.

When she saw the slightly blurred image of the man, she realized she hadn't included him as a possibility at all.

It couldn't be him.

Lily faced her service weapon down.

"Cook, go to your bed."

Cook listened. He went to his bed with a whine but settled.

It wasn't as easy for Lily. Her heartbeat had gone from an even keel to an all-out run. It thumped so hard in her chest she bet her shirt moved.

There was no way it was him.

Right?

Lily opened the door as if it was the first time she'd ever done so. Her inner voice was in total disbelief.

"Ant?"

It had been fourteen years since Anthony Perez had been close enough to touch. The time between felt like a lifetime and it felt like a minute. There was the man—and, goodness, what a man he was—standing on her front doorstep, dripping rain water onto the space where she needed a welcome mat. He was tall but broad, with well-defined muscles she guessed from the way his clothes fit him. The dark hair that had blended in with the night was longer and his face was covered in matching stubble and there was a look to him that let anyone with good eyesight know he wasn't some teenager anymore.

Yet, that was what Lily felt wash over her next. That familiar feeling of standing across from a teenaged Ant. Eyes dark and wild, chaotic energy barely contained in the way he moved and spoke. A boy who was on the cusp of being a man, despite the fact that they'd both been through more than most adults would ever experience.

Ant, the brother.

Ant, the broken.

Ant, the boy drowning in the creek.

There were just some things that time couldn't change—no matter if it was a minute or fourteen years.

For Lily, she was standing in front of a man and seeing the face of a boy in her lap, coughing up water and trying to make sense of the dark world around him.

The logical part of her brain knew that not only was he now a man, he was a man who that morning hadn't been in Kelby Creek.

"What are you doing here?"

Ant hadn't been smiling. He looked even unhappier now.

"What do you mean, *why am I here*?" His tenor caught her off guard, despite having heard it over the phone. It was brass and grit and so distinctly Ant Perez. It also sent a small shiver through her. She didn't have the time to figure out why.

"You're the one who called me about a new lead," he

continued, all pointed syllables. "What was I supposed to do? Just sit around and wait for you to call again?"

Shiver or no shiver, fourteen years or not, Lily jutted out her hip in exasperation.

"Yes! Exactly that."

Ant shook his head. Water shucked off him.

"No way," he shot back. "I don't think so. You can't just call after all these years with a possible new lead and not expect me to run back here, ready to help. I'm part of this."

A boom of thunder put Lily further on edge.

"I said I thought I found a potential lead and that I'd call the moment I knew something," she countered. "I told you I'd keep you updated, not loop you into the investigation. I definitely didn't say for you to come back to Kelby Creek and directly to my home."

Lily's words were professional, analytical.

It was the only way she could handle seeing Ant in person.

Flip the emotional switch was her mantra when it came to work.

And when it came to what happened in the woods when they were teens.

She couldn't *feel* or she'd be overwhelmed.

Overwhelmed with guilt and shame and anger.

None of which would do them any good.

Ant didn't seem to be struggling in the holding-back department. His brow drew in, angry. He pointed a finger at her.

"I may not have a badge or some fancy desk at the department but this is *my* case, Lily. She was my sister. My responsibility. That makes anything new about this case something I need to know. So I'm here. And I'm not leaving town until you can prove to me that the lead is a dead end." His gaze switched to over her shoulder. It seemed to cool Ant a little. His anger transformed into stubbornness. That old familiar chaotic energy was swirling out of him as his parting words came out low and hard.

"I'll be back in the morning, and every morning, until then."

Chapter Three

Anthony was heated going back to his old Camaro at the curb. He could feel it beneath the collar of his shirt and in the tips of his fingers when opening the driver's side door.

Heat.

All-consuming heat.

It always happened when something about Ida's case didn't go his way. Not that there was a right way for it to go. There would never be a right way. Whatever answers he'd eventually get, Ant was realistic enough to know what the outcome would be.

Ida hadn't been seen in fourteen years.

No trace. No hints or even rumors about her or the man who had taken her.

Nothing.

She was gone. Ant knew it, Lily knew it, but that didn't mean he was going to stop looking for the who and why of it all.

Looking for justice.

Looking for vengeance.

Ant turned over his engine and sped out of the neighborhood, a feral growl of frustration mixing in with the rain beating against his windshield. He took a left at the first stoplight and parked in the lot for Rosewater Inn.

He stared at the neon open sign in the bar portion's window.

"Drinking isn't going to solve anything," he told himself. "It's just gonna give you a tab and a headache in the morning. That's all."

Anthony took a deep breath. He sank back in his seat when he let it out.

He hadn't expected his first in-person with Lily in years to go the way it had. After her call about a potential lead he had felt a pull back to town that was so strong that he'd up and left a half hour after their call had ended.

A pull from her.

A pull to the past.

Anthony had expected that to be met with some kind of feeling from Lily. He hadn't expected her to not want him there a lick. Every bit of her looked twisted at the sight of him. It had made his own twisted insides tighten.

He'd walked up that sidewalk to her front porch with each step collecting something new to feel.

The first step had excitement pulsing through his body. They had something. It was a potential lead. A path they hadn't traveled down yet. Not back then, not since. Something new.

Then that excitement turned to something heavy. He was about to see the only other person who understood what it had been like that night in the woods by the creek. Shared trauma and tragedy and commiseration he'd never been able to get from another person in fourteen years.

The nerves had set in next. A few steps of wading through the reality that Lily had obviously been doing things in her life that he hadn't. She'd taken her experience and turned it into a career of helping others. He'd…gone down a different path. One he wasn't always proud of.

Would she see that in him?

Would she look down her nose at his mistakes?

Those nerves had then melted into an anxiousness that had been a powder keg with a quickly burning fuse.

And when Lily had opened the door?

Anthony had felt everything all at once.

Shame, excitement, anxiety, pain, and then utter appreciation.

Lily Howard wasn't just all grown up, she was all grown up and beautiful.

Her hair was longer but still the caramel swirl of light brown and reddish-blond that framed a teardrop face full of focus, freckles, and with eyes that were the color of the forest beneath the moonlight. She was still well below his height but the way she held herself had been more noticeable. More prominent and filled with confidence. Lily Howard wasn't a woman that blended in with the crowd.

She was also no longer the girl by the creek, hair hanging down into her face, telling him to breathe while the rain danced around them.

She was a woman who hadn't wanted him there.

Something about that had been too much. He'd been rude because of it. Abrasive. He'd all but ambushed her. There was no way around it. The only reason he'd come to his senses was because of the baby gate at the bottom of the stairs behind her.

She wasn't the girl by the creek.

She was a woman, at night, standing in her home with a life he was interrupting.

Anthony ran a hand through his hair, heat seeping out like a balloon deflating.

His anger, his frustration. He hadn't meant to aim them at her of all people.

He'd apologize tomorrow. When he was outside her home in the morning.

Because no matter what he felt for Lily Howard, Ant was still back in town for Ida.

Ant sat there a few minutes more trying to decide whether to go into the bar or head to the hotel just outside Kelby Creek. It wasn't the greatest place but he didn't need much. He never did. Ant was always acutely aware that what he had was just one more thing Ida never would. It made appreciating the small things easy. It made missing the big things a passing feeling.

The rain lessened after a few minutes. Ant took it as a sign. He started his car again and was hoping the hotel wasn't full up when he pulled out of the lot.

Another sign came his way before he could even turn onto the road.

On the other side of the intersection was none other than Lily in her car. No one was in the passenger seat but she kept turning toward the back. In between the

turn-arounds Ant could see she wasn't exactly riding easy. Her eyebrows were drawn in and her mouth
twisted down. She was focused. And it didn't seem like
a good thing she was focusing on.

Ant waved in her direction but the light turned green
and she was gone the second it did.

She wasn't just driving. She was heading somewhere
with purpose greasing her pedals.

Ant's light turned green a bit later.

He didn't need any more signs.

He pulled out his phone and dialed the number Lily
had called him from earlier that morning.

She didn't pick up.

Ant stared down the straightaway she'd just taken.

Not a car in sight.

Wherever she was going, she was going there fast.

COOK WAS HAVING a good ol' time in the back seat. He
was a dog born to ride in the car. Never was the boy
happier than when he was pressed against worn cloth
and staring outside as the world flashed by. It didn't
matter that it was raining and dark. Or that his human
was in a foul mood.

Lily hadn't handled Ant's sudden appearance with
the most grace. Berating him wouldn't have been her
first choice but, at the same time, she wasn't about to
be talked down to on her own front porch.

Watching him walk away in a well-deserved huff had
only put her in a mood. She'd scrapped her earlier plan
of showering and heading straight to bed and was ready
to head to her office when her phone had gone off. It

had been one of the new hires at the Dawn County Sheriff's Department. A deputy named Sterling Costner. He couldn't find the hole in the ground that Lily and Sheriff Bennet had been pontificating over earlier that day.

Deputy Costner wasn't new to town by any means but he had admitted that his time in that stretch of the woods in Kelby Creek had been limited. He'd looked for the hole, found nothing, looked a little more, then had gotten a call from his wife, Mel. His words were drenched in worry when he admitted that she wasn't just pregnant but the kind of pregnant that had her throwing up most hours of any waking day. He also didn't step around the fact that her seasickness bands that he was supposed to take home to help her were locked in his truck instead. Lily hadn't needed anything past that. Sure, she wasn't jonesing to go out into the woods at night to look for a hole but what else did she have going for her as an alternative?

Nothing but thinking about Ant, Ida and how she hadn't managed to help either.

Lily had assured Sterling that she could more than handle the task and invited her sidekick Cook along for the ride. It would, at the very least, work out some of their excess energy.

Plus, it was no secret that Lily Howard had once known every part of the woods in Kelby Creek. That went double for the creek itself.

The road was a little washed out but she got to the point where she had parked her car earlier without issue. She parked back a little farther than before so her headlights could illuminate what her flashlight couldn't. The trees lit up like an eerie Christmas. Cook whined in the back seat as she parked.

"I'm not leaving you in the car," she assured him as she got out. "Don't worry."

Lily opened up the back door and patted her leg. Cook bounded out in a flash, yipping playfully. She caught his collar and connected his leash to it. Nine times out of ten the leash wouldn't be needed but Lily wasn't taking her chances with the location.

Kelby Creek's woods ate people whole and those they didn't, they spat out with missing pieces.

"I'll let you run wild at the house," she told him after another loud whine. "Here, you're with me."

Cook stayed at her side and followed her and the beam of her flashlight away from the car. The trees around them stood sentry against the rain and wind. The dirt beneath their feet was now a mass of mush. Lily still followed the landscape with ease.

Yet where there was supposed to be a hole, there was nothing but mud and leaves.

Lily blinked down at the spot for a few moments. Her flashlight beam skittered along the ground like a scanner after a tricky barcode. Lily backtracked to the car, checked for the subtle landmarks she'd followed in before—the tree on the other side of the road that must have been struck by lightning, and the dip in the dirt that had been made from water runoff—and then went back to the same spot.

Still no hole.

"I guess someone filled it," she told Cook.

Even as she said the words, Lily didn't like them.

They didn't feel right. They didn't sit right. A creeping feeling trickled down her back. The dark around her, the rain against her slicker and the mud beneath her feet fused together to make a pit in her stomach.

A pit she'd more than felt before.

For all the things Lily knew of the victims in her cold cases, very few of the living knew about what she'd become after Ida's kidnapping. Sure, professionally her life fit neatly on paper. She'd become determined, singularly focused, and driven to law enforcement after a traumatic event.

But personally? Emotionally? That had been a challenge.

She'd gone to counseling at the insistence of her parents and had been treated for post-traumatic stress and triggers. Gotten tips on how to avoid, deal with, and cope with both. She'd had setbacks and breakthroughs and had gotten the okay from her counselor to make it her choice whether to seek further treatment. Years later and that same counselor was why Cook had come into her life. He'd begun training as a PTSD service dog but, due to budget cuts, hadn't completed the training. Still, he was a companion. A smart, well-behaved friend who could pull Lily out of her own head when she went too deep.

Like when she was standing in the darkness. In the rain. In the mud.

Her hand clutched the flashlight. Her heartbeat sped up. The rain became louder, her breathing with it.

"Just because I'm here doesn't mean that he is, too."

Lily spoke the words softly, a mantra that she had

to recite on occasion. Cook, already sensing her rising anxiety, licked her hand. If that didn't work she knew he'd nudge her next, trying to get her to pet him. If that didn't work he'd try to bring her something to play fetch with.

She didn't know what happened if those three methods failed. She'd been lucky enough to snap out of her episodes before finding out.

Lily felt the warmth of Cook's fur against her fingertips. She focused on it.

"Thanks," she said after a moment. "I'm—"

A stick cracked a few feet behind her.

The word *okay* flew back down her throat and ran into her heart there.

She spun around.

It was a man. Or, rather, a silhouette of one standing just inside the beams of her headlights. That silhouette was alarmingly tall. He also had his hands in the air.

The details filtered in next.

Dark hair, a low-slung vehicle parked on the road just behind her car.

Anthony.

"I tried calling," he yelled out. "You weren't answering."

"So you followed me?" Lily's voice cracked. It caught her by surprise. "First my house and now this?"

Ant was nonplussed by her anger. Maybe because it wasn't true anger at all. Her heart was still racing and the rain was still loud. He didn't move a muscle.

"I saw you driving and you looked a little freaked.

When I saw you pull in here, I wanted to make sure you were okay."

Lily made a loud noise of strangled frustration.

"I'm fine," she exclaimed, rain running down her nose from the wet tangles of her hair.

Ant was obviously not convinced.

His voice was calm and even when he responded.

"Then why do you still have your gun pointing at me?"

It was as if someone had thrown back a curtain. All at once Lily saw her service weapon aimed at Ant and felt her viselike grip on it and the flashlight she'd tucked beneath the butt.

She hadn't even realized that she'd pulled the weapon out.

"That's what happens when you get surprised by someone stalking you," she responded hotly. Lily returned her weapon to the holster at her hip. "At night. For the second time."

Ant lowered his hands.

At the sound of Cook barking, Lily realized she had dropped his leash when she'd gotten gun-happy.

"Cook, come!"

But the Lab stayed behind her, just outside the trees. He kept barking.

It wasn't at them.

Lily pointed her flashlight's beam down and hurried over. Cook's nose was in the dirt.

Right where the hole was supposed to be.

"What is it?" Ant appeared at her side, eyes on the ground.

"There was a hole here earlier today. Someone called it in but we didn't find anything weird other than the hole itself. The sheriff wanted us to come back out and check on it." Lily crouched down. Cook was insistent on something. He wasn't just touching the dirt. He was nosing it hard enough that it was displacing. More concerning was he hadn't even alerted to Ant's presence. "I came out here because the deputy that was supposed to check on it couldn't find it."

Lily placed the flashlight on the ground. She put her hand on the damp dirt. This only seemed to rally Cook. He started digging with his front paws.

That feeling, that pit in her stomach, started to tighten.

Her body must have registered something her mind hadn't yet caught up to. Lily lowered her head and turned her ear to the ground.

It was only the second after she'd done it that she understood why.

"I—I can hear something."

The world around her seemed to fade away.

Then she heard it again.

A scream.

Muffled, but definitely a scream.

And it was coming from beneath her hand.

Lily looked up, ice filling her veins.

"Anthony, I think someone's buried under here."

Chapter Four

Ant had big hands. Big, calloused hands from manual labor and years of hard work. When he left Kelby Creek, he didn't set out to pursue one single trade. He just aimed to survive for a while. Survive until he could find the truth. Then, maybe, he could start really living.

There was also real power behind his hands. Years of surviving came right up along years of preparing.

He'd made a promise to himself the day after Ida had been taken.

He wouldn't give another attacker the satisfaction of besting him in a fight and he certainly would never again be that boy with his eyes closed in the creek water.

In the end it all added up to big, strong hands ready for anything.

That included digging into the wet earth.

Ant plunged his fingers down into the mud and threw back the dirt, knees sinking down into the ground a little with each handful. Lily was right beside him, digging in a frenzied rush. Even her dog was doing his part.

It wasn't long before he hit something hard.

Anthony's fingers stubbed against the immovable object less than a foot down.

"Flashlight!"

Lily moved the beam over his shoulder and into the hole they'd made.

Ant brushed the dirt aside. "It's wood."

Lily's hair brushed against his shoulder as she peered over into the circle of light.

"That wasn't here this morning."

On cue another scream sounded.

This time he could make out a word.

"Help!"

Anthony dug back in, scooping out the dirt until the wood stopped.

"It's a box," he yelled. "She's buried in a box!"

Lily dropped back to her knees as they furiously tried to move more dirt aside to open the top of the container. Ant could make out one hinge on the side but the top had no openings. No handles. He ran his fingers along where there should have been a lip, looking for a latch or something he could undo to open it.

There was nothing.

If the box opened, it wasn't from the direction they were looking down on.

"We're going to have to break it open."

He shook his head trying to get a purchase on the corner. There were no slats or holes. Whoever was inside had to be low on oxygen and only getting lower.

"I can't get it," he grunted out.

The wood was firm.

There was nothing he could do with his bare hands.

"I might have something in the car," Lily said. "I'll call this in, too."

Lily was up and running. Her dog went with her, barking.

The rain continued to fall, not caring about their situation.

"Hang on," Ant yelled down to the woman in the box. "We'll get this open!"

Ant got lower and threw all of his strength into digging out one side. It wasn't a successful move. There was no way he could dig it out by hand in time. He needed a shovel. The box had to have been standing straight up. That meant if there was a latch on the side or the bottom it would be a while before they could get to it.

A while the woman probably didn't have.

"Can you hear me?" he called out.

He waited for the woman to answer.

She just kept screaming for help.

It was a haunting sound.

Ant tried to pull at the box again. He slipped and a splinter tore into his hand.

"Hurry, Lily!"

Ant balled his fist. If they couldn't find something to break into it, he'd have to make his fists do the job. A few broken knuckles was a worthy price to pay for freeing someone buried alive.

He flexed his hand, ready, but Lily's dog's barks became noticeably louder.

Then the growling started.

Ant spun around at the sound. So did Lily right next to the car.

Together they saw what her dog was alerting them to.

It was the only reason she had time to throw herself to the side as a man in a yellow rain slicker lunged at her, a shovel swinging down in his hand.

LILY DIDN'T HAVE time to make a noise. She barely had time to move as the shovel crashed into the ground next to her. The wind from the swing was as unsettling as Cook's snarling.

Lily's shoulder connected with the ground as she went down. Her cheek hit the dirt next. There wasn't even a breath of time to dwell on the pain as her attacker recovered instantly from his missed hit.

He swung the shovel back up like a human pendulum and put the force of both hands around the wood. It was going to be a devastating blow, no matter where it hit her. Lily struggled to move enough so that the shovel wouldn't be the last thing she saw. With the heels of her boots she tried to push herself backward.

The mud was unforgiving.

One boot slipped along the wet ground and that was enough. She lost her only opening to avoid a painful fate. And the attacker knew it. He brought the shovel down with startling quickness.

Somehow it stopped in midair.

In the glow of the flashlight that had fallen to the ground, Ant appeared, his hand wrapped around the wood of the shovel, holding it back with apparent ease.

Lily gaped up at him, awestruck.

He said only one word to the man in the rain slicker before turning the tide.

"No."

The shovel came out of Rain Slicker's hand just as Cook's growls turned into a bite. The man roared in pain. He kicked out on what must have been reflex. Or pragmatism. Fight the thing dealing you current damage, not the thing that's coming next.

And boy, was Ant coming next.

The man kicked out at Cook again. Lily was pulled to her feet by Cook's yelp right as Ant put the mystery man on his tail with a momentum-infused arc of the shovel. The metal thunked against the man's arm with audible force.

He stumbled back. Cook kept his distance but was back to growling.

Ant readied for another swing while Lily went for her gun.

Neither had the chance to follow through.

The man might have been outnumbered but he was deceptively fast. One second he was fighting for footing among the mud, the next he was spinning. He did a 180 and charged Ant.

Momentum won out again. This time not in their favor.

The men collided and hit the ground. Ant made a noise at the impact and the shovel fell to the mud. Rain Slicker started to wail fists against him. Enraged, Lily sprang into action. Instead of going for the gun and possibly shooting the very man she was trying to help, Lily scooped up the shovel.

It only seemed fair since she was the only one who hadn't used it yet.

Thunder clapped overhead, rain kept falling, and Lily brought the shovel down on their attacker's back like she was gunning for a prize at the fair.

He roared in pain. Gut-twisting, can't-get-out-of-your-head pain.

Lily tried to use that pain. She went for his wrist to attempt a pin. Ant seemed to pick up on the attempt and tried to flip the man, grunting at the effort.

But once again, Rain Slicker was a surprise and a half.

He pulled Lily forward. The second she fell was the second he threw a punch.

Pain lit up behind her eyes as his fist collided with her jaw. She clenched her teeth, willing herself not to pass out, but she knew she was going to feel it in the morning.

Ant made an ugly noise and charged the attacker, connecting several blows. The man in the slicker became the man on his back.

After a few more hits the man went limp, his hands slapping the wet ground beneath him.

Lily held her breath, waiting for another attack.

It didn't come.

Instead Cook ran up and licked at her cheek.

"Are you okay?" Ant looked down to meet Lily's eyes. There was blood dripping down from his eyebrow and lip.

Lily shook herself. "Yeah. Yeah, I'm okay. You?"

Ant nodded but he wasn't staying put long.

"He's out. Can you restrain him with something? Cuffs or ties?"

Lily reached out and touched Cook. He seemed okay, too.

She nodded.

"I have ties in my car."

Ant pushed himself off the ground and grabbed the discarded shovel. He ran over back to their original goal.

The woman buried in the box.

Lily struggled to her feet. She threw Cook into the back seat and shut the car door quickly behind the dog. She backtracked to where she'd dropped her phone when Rain Slicker had first attacked. Their night dispatcher, Janet Kim, took her hurried call in stride. A marvel considering she'd already called in their earlier situation and that had been dire enough.

"I need both hands so I'm hanging up," she told Janet. "The guy in yellow is the baddie. Don't touch the man with the black hair."

Lily ended the call and grabbed the crowbar from her trunk. Her ties came next.

She made quick work of hog-tying Rain Slicker before binding his hands and feet. The adrenaline from the fight started to fade as she went through the motions. It ushered in more pain. It also put an extra urgency on the noise behind her. If she was hurting, she couldn't imagine what the woman in the box was going through.

A shovel biting into dirt. A man grunting with exertion. Rain continuing to make the effort more difficult.

Ant trying to save a woman who Rain Slicker must not have wanted saved.

Lily bypassed the urge to do more than a quick search to see that he wasn't carrying any weapons and high-tailed it to Ant. It was amazing how much he'd shoveled out around the box in the short time she'd been at the car.

"This thing opens from the side," he huffed at her as he dug and flung the dirt over his shoulder. The blood on his face mixed with the rain but the dripping water could not wash away his determined expression. "Like a coffin standing up. It's gonna be hard to break open without being dug all the way out."

But that didn't stop him from trying. Ant took the crowbar after digging out some more space. He'd uncovered, she guessed, half of the box. True to his own guess, there was an obvious gap that ran up to the corner next to the top. It was a lid.

Ant jammed the head of the crowbar into the small opening.

"Move away from my voice," he yelled out to the woman inside. "I'm breaking the box!"

He pushed against the bar. Nothing happened for a moment. Then the wood made a cracking sound.

Lily grabbed the shovel and put the metal blade into the small opening the crowbar was making. When it caught, she also started to push against it. For a moment that was all they did.

Using leverage and gravity to try to break the box open while a woman screamed for help over and over again.

Not at all what Lily had expected of the night.

Not at all what she'd expected to deal with during her career.

That didn't mean she felt any less grateful when the slow cracking became a fast break.

The box splintered open at the top, breaking at the force of their tools. Lily fell back onto the dirt outside the hole. Ant went in the other direction. He dropped the crowbar and started pulling at the remaining wood with his bare hands.

The next board wasn't as quick to snap but it eventually gave way. Lily scrambled over to see into the new opening, ready to assess how hurt the woman was, who she was, and to assure her that she was all right.

But when Ant pulled back the board, the yelling didn't skip a beat.

Which was confusing, considering there was no woman in the box at all.

"What in the—" Ant reached his hand through the opening and snaked it downward. He got a hold of something and pulled it back out, hands covered in dirt, rain and blood.

The woman's yells were louder now.

Ant turned to her, holding something slightly bigger than his hand up in the rain between them. The screams for help were coming out of it with a crispness that was disarming.

Lily took the object from Ant's hand.

"It's a tape recorder," she said. "The play button is taped down. It's on a loop."

Ant looked from it and then back to the box.

His voice was loud and angry when he spoke.

"What the hell is going on here?"

Chapter Five

Ant was leaning against the break room counter, Cook lying asleep at his feet. Lily Howard was standing tall and absolutely in her element, though soaked to the bone.

"I need to question our attacker. I have a list of questions I want answered," she told Detective Foster Lovett. A man who Ant was actually familiar with but hadn't seen since they were teens. "And that's why I want to investigate this," Lily continued, her voice as even as a tightrope. "I'm motivated to find the answers."

Foster opened his mouth to probably buck Lily's demand again but paused when a dark-skinned woman with a round, very pregnant belly walked in. Ant recognized her from a story in the local paper a few years back. It was Millie, Foster's wife. Someone else who had dealt with a sibling disappearing.

Lucky for both of them they'd gotten a happy ending.

Millie had a small bag of ice packs she'd gotten from the drugstore. The gel kind that felt nice no matter how bad a shiner you were rocking. Millie handed him the biggest of the bunch. He nodded to her but then handed it to Lily. She took it without a word, her eyes still on Foster. Ant took a smaller pack for his eyebrow. It had stopped bleeding but he knew his skin was still stained from it.

"You're going to give a statement but you aren't going to talk to him now," Foster stated when Lily pressed the pack to her jaw. "You're dripping wet, bloodied and tired. We can handle questioning the guy. Detective Reiner is already at the site with Sheriff Bennet. You can go home and tomorrow we can go over your questions."

"We were there from go to stop," Ant piped up. "Lily should be asking that guy questions before any of you even introduce yourselves. Sidelining her because she's got mud on her boots and a little blood on her clothes makes as much sense as a recorder being buried in a box."

Lily didn't look at him but Ant saw her give a little nod. Foster wasn't convinced.

"We have protocols that we need to stick to now," he tried again. "Ones that go into effect after a law enforcement–involved altercation."

"I wasn't on the clock," Lily said.

Foster shook his head. "Doesn't mean you're a civilian. And it doesn't mean we're going to let you talk to the man." Foster pinched his nose and sighed. "Go home. Come back in the morning. That's the best I'm going to do, especially since our perp is currently being evaluated at the hospital. Instead of rattling around here, waiting, at least get that dog a bone and yourself some dry clothing. Okay?"

Ant knew that Lily wasn't happy with her options but she gave a curt nod all the same.

"Do I need to call Detective Gray or have you already notified him?" Lily's voice had changed a little but Ant couldn't figure out which end of the emotional spectrum it had gone toward.

Foster nodded. "We were actually with him and his wife, Willa, when I got the call. He'll be here bright and early tomorrow, too."

If there was any more hesitation in Lily, it seemed to leave at that. Ant pushed off the counter and whistled. Cook was up and alert in a flash. His tail was wagging as they followed Lily out.

"I need to go by my office really quick," she said over her shoulder. Ant turned with her and soon they were in a somewhat large room with three desks, several filing cabinets and a few boxes neatly organized.

Lily glanced back at the door. She went to one of the two desks butted up against each other and bent low. Ant got the impression that whatever she was doing, she didn't want the head detective or his wife to see. He stepped back to block the door. Cook sat next to him, tail still wagging.

Lily pulled an accordion folder from a drawer. She tucked it under her arm, despite still being wet from the rain. Ant eyed her desk as she looked in another drawer. The top was neat. Just an orderly set of pens and a computer monitor.

That was it.

No framed pictures. No knickknacks.

Just order.

It fit her.

"All right. I'm ready."

Lily was pressing the folder tight against her while they made their exit out of the sheriff's department. She didn't offer any explanation when they stopped next to her car in the parking lot and let Cook into the back seat.

He wasn't going to pry.

Not after the night they'd had.

"That's a good dog," Ant said instead. "He was one heck of an alarm and then a fighting buddy when we needed him."

Lily was hovering between their cars. She nodded but it was easy to see she wasn't all there. The parking lot's lone light showed a woman with a jaw that was bruised and wet hair that was dark from the rain. Ant reached out, ducking his chin down a little for a better angle to see the other mark on her cheek. He skimmed the scratched area with his thumb, careful not to apply too much pressure.

"I guess getting the equivalent of rug burn from the ground is better than getting a shovel to the back," he reasoned. Then he made a face. "But still, I'm not happy seeing it. Does it sting?"

Lily took a step back, just out of reach. She shook her head.

"Only when I focus on it so I'm not going to focus on it. What about you?" She didn't touch him, or even reach for him. Her eyes were the only thing that moved.

"I've had much worse than a busted lip and a split eyebrow before. Nothing some more ice and maybe a beer can't handle."

If Lily had been someone else, maybe a woman he'd dated in the past, he thought she might follow up to make sure he wasn't putting on a brave face. But Lily was, well, Lily. She took him at his word. The silence that followed didn't leave a nice taste in his mouth, though. He broke it quickly.

"I think it's a load of crock you aren't at the hospital now, talking to that guy," he said. "You've already proven you can handle yourself. Plus, we found the box and, considering he had the shovel, I'm assuming he dug the hole. Not hard math for anyone, and baby stuff for a detective like you."

Ant thought he saw a smile try to show itself on her face. He wasn't sure if it was his imagination or not. Either way, Lily made a noise that sounded dangerously close to contempt.

"I'm too emotionally close to this," she said. "Sometimes it's hard to keep yourself in line during something like this. It was the right call. Even if we don't like it."

Ant thought of Ida.

He knew Lily went there, too.

If she was too emotionally invested in the man in the slicker and the buried box, what did that mean for Ida's investigation? Had Lily stripped out her feelings for what had happened? Had she moved on but was just trying to see it through for him?

Ant could have asked her—he could have asked her several times over throughout the years—but, like always, he kept his mouth shut.

They could talk about Ida's case but they never talked about what happened. Not in detail. Not about the creek.

He wasn't going to start now.

Lily sighed. She wrung out her hair over her shoulder.

"It's late," she said. "And Foster isn't wrong. We're all in dire need of a change and a shower. Everything else we can talk about tomorrow. Where are you staying?"

Ant had been thinking about a hotel earlier. Now his mind went to the Camaro.

"It's between a hotel and my car," he said, honestly. "I'm not picky about where I sleep and I'm not sure I'm up to driving out of Kelby Creek tonight."

He refrained from telling her that he really wasn't up for leaving her. Ant could no more get the image of the man bringing down the shovel on Lily out of his head than he could bring himself to call the hotel to see if there were any vacancies. Instead he shrugged. It wasn't a big deal to sleep in his car. He'd done it before.

"What about your cousin?" Lily asked. "Don't you normally stay with her when you come to town?"

It surprised Ant that Lily knew he came to town on occasion. Then again, hadn't they talked on the phone a few years back when he'd been with Shandra? Maybe her memory was just that good. Ant did get the feeling that Lily had a knack for being detail-oriented. It was part of the job, right?

He nodded. The pain in his brow throbbed at the movement.

"I do but it's a full house now that her father-in-law is bunking there along with the kids. I don't want to get in the way, especially since I didn't call ahead and it's late."

Lily eyed him in a way she hadn't before. Like she

was tallying up invisible data. She cocked her head to the side a little.

"If you don't mind bunking on my couch, you can stay with me tonight," she said, simply. "Me and Cook, that is. He sleeps in a crate in my room so he wouldn't bother you."

Ant wanted to say that there was nothing that Cook could do to bother him after what the dog had done out in the woods. Instead he asked if she was sure.

"I really don't mind hanging in my car," Ant added. "You were right earlier. You didn't ask for me to come to town and you definitely weren't expecting me, either."

He recalled the baby gate at the stairs. He also, not for the first time, tried to peek at her hand to see if a ring was on it, but Lily nodded and that was that.

"You stopped a shovel from ruining my day. Offering my couch is the least I can do."

Ant ignored the excitement that stirred in him. He wasn't in Kelby Creek for Lily, after all. Only for her lead. Her small lead she hadn't explained to him yet.

Now he wouldn't have to wait on her doorstep in the morning for that conversation.

Now all he had to do was wake up in her living room.

That's why he was excited.

Right?

"Okay, then," he said after a moment. "Lead the way."

COOK WASN'T THE only one shaking off when they were stopped at the garage door leading into the house. Lily's clothes were still soaked and her jeans had adhered to her skin by means of mud. Both had her feeling all kinds of ick. Cook, though, didn't seem to mind his new weight. His tail was wagging as he nosed the door.

"If you think for a second that I'm going to let you run around wearing all of that mud, you have another think coming, buddy."

Lily slid her rain jacket off and hung it up on one of the hooks next to the door. She took her boots off next, deciding the wet socks would just have to stay in the garage for the night. Her hair was already up in a messy bun and she was sure the light makeup she'd been wearing was now washed away. She rolled her neck around to dispel some of the tension and started to slip her fingers under the hem of her shirt. She caught herself before she could lift it over her stomach.

For once, she wasn't alone.

A car door shut in the distance. The security light outside the garage came to life.

Ant made his way through the circle of light with a backpack. It was the only thing he was wearing from his waist up.

He was just a man in his jeans and shoes, bloodied and bruised.

And looking every bit as strong as Lily had suspected him to be.

His torso didn't move as he walked up to meet her. It was a wall of hardened muscle.

She wasn't exactly sure what all Anthony Perez had been up to over the past fourteen years but she'd put money on the fact that he definitely worked out.

"My shirt didn't even make the drive. I had to chuck

it in the parking lot trash can before I followed you," he explained, motioning to his chest.

Lily felt her face heat. She adjusted her gaze to the key ring in her hand and cleared her throat. Then tried to play it off as a small cough. She wasn't sure if she hit the mark.

"I'm definitely going to have to start a new load of laundry ASAP if I have any hope of saving mine." Cold air burrowed into her wet clothes as the door to the house opened. It was all Cook needed to begin his own personal race. He was off into the dark house with excited yips and the sound of nails on hardwood. "I'm also going to have to give that one a bath before he destroys the house!"

Cook had the zoomies. There was no denying that. He went from lapping up some water from his bowl in the kitchen to running full speed into the living room. Despite the pain pulsing through various parts of her body, Lily had to give chase.

"Crap! I forgot to put up the gate! He's going to go straight to my bed!"

Lily followed the Lab through the hall, around a quick loop in the guest bathroom, and was hot on his heels when he barked excitedly through the living room. She was already imagining the additional laundry she'd have to do once the mud-covered dog rocketed himself onto her clean bed.

"Not so fast there, buddy!"

Ant was at the foot of the stairs, crouched and with his arms held open wide. The baby gate was secured behind him, blocking the steps.

Cook crashed into him, giving off a stray bark for good measure. Despite the gate, the dog couldn't have been happier to have a fresh face to lick. His tail thudded against the hardwood like a ticking clock.

Lily took a second to catch her breath, listening to Ant laugh at the dog trying to lap up his face.

"Thanks," Lily breathed out. "You just saved my bedspread."

"Not a problem." Ant found a good spot behind Cook's ear to scratch. "Want me to help you corral him into the bathroom?"

Lily wasn't going to say it but she was surprised at Cook's trust in Ant, a relative stranger. Maybe it had to do with the fact that Ant had helped them in the fight.

Either way Lily was grateful for the offer. Together they got Cook into the guest bathroom without any fuss. Lily motioned to upstairs when they were settled.

"You can take the baby gate down and head upstairs to the bathroom for your own shower," she offered. "Cook is a great dog but this might take a bit."

"You sure? I don't mind helping."

"You've already helped a lot tonight," she said with a quick shake of her head. "Showering is your reward."

Ant laughed and the motion lit up his eyes. It was quite the contrast to his bloodied eyebrow and split lip. As they'd wrestled with Cook a moment ago, she'd finally caught a glimpse of his knuckles, busted and caked in blood, and wanted nothing more than for him to rest.

"All right. I won't be long. Reward or not, I'm not a shower hog."

He disappeared upstairs while Cook received a quick but thorough bath. Lily brushed her hand over his fur and skin and examined both. As far as she could tell there were no injuries from their attacker. Still, it boiled her blood and hurt her soul to hear her dog whimper during the fight. Had she known there was even a remote possibility that going to check on the hole would lead to him being in danger...

Lily dropped the towel she'd been using to dry the dog. She buried her head in the fur of his neck.

"You're definitely sleeping with me tonight, wet or not," she whispered.

Cook just kept wagging his tail.

Lily emerged from the bathroom, exhausted. Cook went to the baby gate and sat down next to it, as if he knew what she'd just offered. Ant was already back in the living room, this time with a shirt on.

The bruising on his face was easier to see now that he was cleaned up.

Lily wasn't a fan of it, either. She wanted to say something, a lot of something, but the world of what had happened between them felt too large.

And she was tired.

"I'll grab some blankets and pillows," was all she said before going to the linen closet.

Ant was quiet when she handed them over. He stayed quiet when she finally spoke.

"Help yourself to any food, drink or ice packs in the kitchen. I'm going to shower now and try to get some sleep. You should, too."

Ant stared at her for a second. No words, just dark eyes on her.

Lily saw him standing there one second, then saw him stopping the shovel in the next.

"No."

It would have sent a shiver through her had she not felt her body being dragged down by pain and the need to rest.

She also didn't want to think about what would have happened had he not been there. If she'd been caught by the man, alone.

Then, as it often did, the present dissolved into a memory of the past.

Ant wasn't in Kelby Creek to save her.

And Lily could tell that he'd remembered that fact, too.

Ant's words were low but calm. He took a step forward, the pillow still in his hand.

"We've had a night of it, I'll give you that, but the world could stop spinning and it wouldn't keep me from asking about her. About Ida. You of all people should know that."

Lily did. She said as much.

"I do."

Ant took another step closer. As if being near her would help transfer what she knew right into him.

"This morning you said you had a potential lead and then you asked me if I remembered Ida's abductor coughing when we were in the woods." He shook his head a little. His stare never wavered from her. "You've asked me a lot of questions through the years…but you've never asked me that. Why? What changed?"

Lily didn't want to answer; she didn't want to lie. So she simplified her response, for brevity's sake.

"A man named Bryant Lautner was pulled over for speeding an hour before Ida was taken. The deputy let him go with a warning because he couldn't stop coughing and the deputy didn't want to get sick." Lily felt the slight adrenaline surge she'd gotten when first reading the report. The memory of that horrible night pushed in next. "When we first chased after the man and Ida into the woods, I couldn't find them for a second. It was too dark. The rain was in my eyes. But then I heard him coughing. That's how I knew which direction to run in."

If Ant had been sitting, Lily bet dollars to doughnuts he would have jumped up at that. His entire body went taut. Cook alerted to him with a nudge at his hand.

"And this Bryant Lautner, where is he now?"

Lily held up her hands to stop him. He had already jumped down the rabbit hole, no questions asked. She didn't need that from him. Not right now.

"That's what I've been trying to find out. You were going to be my first call after I did."

Ant's look of skepticism stung at that. He didn't believe her.

She wasn't sure she believed her, either.

It was such a small lead and they'd been burned before. If she hadn't needed his answer—to know if he remembered the man coughing for reassurance that she was remembering right—Lily might not have included Ant in it at all.

Why give him the burden of reliving the heartbreak of losing his sister all over again? She hadn't wanted to, unless it was necessary.

Right now, it wasn't.

Before he could wind up, Lily walked to the stairs.

"I'll see you in the morning, Ant," she said, voice hard. "Try to get some sleep."

She was done talking. By the look in his eye, he knew it, too. He accepted it but not without his lips deepening into a frown.

"You too."

His voice was far-off.

Lily went up the stairs. A world of pain and memories stretched between them.

She doubted either one of them would get a good sleep tonight.

Chapter Six

The sheets were cold. Smooth and cold.

Light from the hallway plug-in reached through the space of the open door. The blackout curtains were doing their job, though the darkness from the rain hitting the roof above definitely helped.

Lily rolled over and stretched her hand out. There was no fur or wiggle of warmth next to her. She opened her eyes wider and tried to focus in the mostly dark room.

Cook wasn't on the bed.

She rolled over and peered down at his crate. She'd left it open the night before in case Cook wanted to fall into routine. Then she'd promptly fallen asleep with him at her side. He wasn't in either spot now.

Which meant he was downstairs.

And so was Ant.

Lily's stomach tightened on reflex.

Anthony Perez was in her house. On her couch. All these years later.

She didn't know how to feel about that. So she switched her focus to something she understood well.

Pain.

There was throbbing in various places across her body. Most notably her shoulder. Nothing was broken but everything felt bruised. Her muddy romp with Rain Slicker had indeed left a mark.

Lily felt along her nightstand until she found the bottle of ibuprofen. She took two with a sip from a water bottle before even sitting up all the way.

If she was in pain, she had to guess Ant was swimming in it.

Lily padded to the small en suite bathroom and went through her morning routine. She pulled half of her hair up and dressed in a white tank top, a pair of black jeans and a blazer. She was deeply fond of the coat given how lightweight it was in the Southern humidity and the fact that it hid her shoulder holster well. Lily's boots were still in the garage so she left the room in her socks. She felt weirdly naked doing so.

She also felt bare without lipstick on so she put that on, too.

Then she stopped by her dresser to rub it off on her discarded sleep shirt.

She was about to see Anthony Perez. Not go on some date.

Lily straightened her blazer and checked her phone. Six thirty. One unread text.

It was from Detective Gray. The time stamp was right after midnight.

I'll be in the office at start of shift. If you need time off, take it.

Lily wasn't going to accept that offer. There was no need for her to skip out on interrogating their attacker. She only hoped the big bosses agreed. If not, maybe bringing Ant with her wouldn't be such a bad idea. He *had* defended her the night before. And he hadn't just been talking. He'd believed what he was saying. She deserved to be in there more than the rest. She could handle her own, after all.

It was nice to hear the confidence. In her last job the bullpen had been male-dominated and, of those men, several had shown animosity toward her, a younger woman well on her way up the ladder. Fighting for her spot, her right, wasn't something she liked doing. Though she would, it had still been a good feeling to hear someone standing behind her, defending her.

It was still such a bizarre feeling to know that it had been Ant's voice rallying her.

They weren't even friends, really. Apart from a few conversations over the phone through the years, they hadn't spoken with much depth to each other. Hadn't made plans to catch up. Didn't talk about anything that wasn't Ida-related.

They were just two people who had shared an awful day together. One that had obviously followed them into the lives they'd led since.

But as she descended the stairs, careful not to make too much noise, she couldn't help but want to know more. How had he left North Carolina so fast? Did his boss understand? Did his girlfriend, if he had one, care? Had he listened to music on the ride down or was he an audiobook kind of guy? Maybe he'd taken to podcasts, playing them off his phone as he ate up the miles.

Or had he used the road and silence to think about the woods? The creek?

Lily misjudged her attention span. With her thoughts on Ant she forgot to step lightly on the second-to-last step on the stairs. Its whine was as loud as it was unforgiving. Lily cringed and braced for Cook to round the corner and a sleepy Ant to wake, but neither the dog nor the man made a peep. Curious, she walked around the corner.

Ant was lying across the couch, with his elbows propped up and a phone in his hands. The space between his cell and the blanket strewn across his hips housed a black Lab.

Lily couldn't help but give a little laugh at the sight.

"And here I thought no one would ever replace me in the eyes of Cook the Lab."

Cook's tail wagged in sync with Ant's laughter. He set down his phone as the dog scrambled off him and toward her.

"I hope it's okay that he's up here. I kind of patted my chest when he was coming back from using the bathroom and then it was game over."

Lily gave Cook a good scratch. She snorted.

"To be fair, he's somewhat of a clingy dog. The pat probably wasn't needed."

Ant was sitting up now. Once again he was shirtless. Lily made sure to rein her focus to his face. A task made easier considering the state of it.

"How's your—" Lily motioned to all of her face.

Ant smirked. He fingered the scab over his eyebrow. "Again, not the worst scrapes I've gotten through the years. Hurts a little, will look cooler if it scars. If not I'm sure it'll be fine in a few days." Those dark eyes moved to Lily's cheek. She was glad for the distance between them. "What about you? Your jaw isn't bruising like I thought it might. How's the cheek?"

Lily had already examined her injuries in the mirror while getting ready. He was right, the punch she'd taken to the jaw hadn't left as much of a bruise as it could have. Didn't mean it hurt less but it was nice that the wound wasn't noticeable. The scrape on her cheek was another story. It was a kiss of red with some light scabbing. If she'd felt so inclined, she might have covered it with some foundation.

"Neither really hurt," she decided to say. "Would be cool if it scars but if not I'll be okay in a few days."

Ant wasn't distracted by her humor. He stood and crossed his arms over his chest.

"But something's bothering you," he guessed. "Something hurts. I can tell by how you're holding yourself. What is it?"

Lily sighed. She was going to have to get a better poker face for her entire body.

"My shoulder." She shrugged the one in question. It hurt. Plain and simple. "You'd think all the rain we've had would have softened the ground a little. I hit it when I first went to the ground avoiding the shovel." Ant's own body language betrayed him. He was readying to close the distance between them again. Lily didn't want that. She started to walk toward the kitchen to avoid the closeness. "I already took some meds, though. Right now I could really do with some coffee. Do you want some?"

The coffee maker was perhaps the most used appliance in the house. It was a single-cup and had been bought for the express purpose of trying to limit how much caffeine she consumed in a day. That had been a woefully unachieved goal. Lily found comfort in the smell of it, the feel of the mug in her hand, the routine. The actual taste ranked last in things she craved from the drink. Lily was searching for that constant now. She opened her cupboard and selected one of her travel mugs.

She hadn't said so, but she wasn't planning on sticking around long that morning.

Ant found a way to break the routine by way of a simple comment.

"I remember seeing your dad out on your front porch every morning with a mug like that in his hand." He was leaning against the counter, just as he had at the station. Unbothered. Yet forever haunted. A combination that shouldn't work but did for him.

Lily felt a flash of envy. He was so easy to be with and she…had to run to the coffeepot to avoid the world.

"He always tipped his head and cup to me when I was on the way to school." Ant mimicked the motion. That flash of envy Lily had felt now turned into a smoldering ache. She hoped she hid the change. She tried to smile into the memories.

"Do you know that he made a cup every morning, came home to get a cup at lunch, and then had another one right after dinner?" Lily placed her own mug beneath the dispenser. She mirrored Ant's stance against the counter next to her. "As a kid I wondered how he fell asleep after all that caffeine. As an adult in law enforcement I wonder how he stopped at three cups a day."

Ant laughed. It wasn't as boisterous as she was finding his normal trill was.

"My cousin Shandra told me a while back that they moved, your parents," he ventured. "How are they doing?"

Lily held back that emotional switch in perfect stillness.

"Good. They moved right before I went to college. Up to a place called Beaver Creek, New York, if you can believe it." Ant's eyebrow rose high at that. "Dad lived there in his teens and fell in love with the place. Once I was out of the house for good they decided it was as good a time as any." She bit down hard on the rest of the truth—her parents had told her they were leaving before she'd actually gone to school. Most longtime locals only left because of The Flood. But not her parents. They had packed up and left their home behind because of her.

Because Lily couldn't stop obsessing over Ida.

You won't be a ghost in our home any longer, her mother had told her one morning, her father's first cup of coffee of the day brewing in the background. *If you won't try to move on by yourself, then we're just going to have to force you to take the first step.*

So they'd gone.

Then so had Lily.

Ant nodded now, unaware of the words she was keeping in. Her own coffee started to pour next to her.

"Mom tried staying for a while," he told her. "She made it a lot longer than I did, but finally moved to El Paso to be with my aunt."

"That's nice," Lily said, honest. She knew his father had passed away when Ida was a baby. That had only made the family that much closer.

Ant agreed.

"We video chat or talk on the phone at least once a week. Her latest kick has been enjoying her time as great-aunt to my cousin Phillipe's new kid. Though that happiness has turned into a very pointed kind of peer pressure." Ant laughed again. His tone had changed once more. It was lighter. "Apparently I was supposed to supply her with a grandchild years ago and I just didn't get the memo."

Lily felt heat in her belly at that. Not a lot but it was there.

"Hey, it could be worse. At least it's your mom pushing you about it and not your girlfriend."

This time the laughter came out in a boom. Ant was grinning hard when it was through.

"Was that your way of fishing to see if I'm dating anyone?" Ant asked, teasing. The heat in her belly became the heat in her face.

"No," she defended. "It was just an observation!"

Ant crossed his arms over his chest.

"I don't think so. In fact, I think Lily Howard, Detective Extraordinaire, was trying to do some snooping."

Lily snorted. She rolled her eyes and went for her cup as the sound of the coffee maker cut off.

"It was *conversation*, not snooping," she returned. "If I was snooping I would have just straight-up asked you if you had some girlfriend up in North Carolina."

Ant was still having fun, laughing behind her.

Again that envy crawled back up to say hi to her. Sometimes Ant could be so easy when she felt so defensive and stiff.

He was brandishing a small smile when she went into the walk-in pantry for Cook's food. It was still turning up the corners of his lips when he guided her out of the way and took the plastic kibble scoop from her.

"Your shoulder is hurt, Detective Howard," he said. "Let me get Cook sorted and you just worry about your coffee."

Lily hesitated for a moment. She relented in the next. Cook let out a yip of excitement the second he heard his food hit the scoop. He wasn't at all patient as he followed Ant to his bowl. If he hadn't already been a fan of the man, that would have cinched it.

Ant moved back through the kitchen and into the pantry again like it was old habit.

"I don't have one, by the way," he called out. "A girlfriend. I did but we broke up last year. What about you?"

Lily hurriedly answered before he could come back out. Not that it needed any great length of time.

"Nope. Just dating my job."

She wasn't embarrassed by her answer but she couldn't deny she was glad at the subject change when he emerged.

"Speaking of, I was thinking about last night." He took a seat opposite her at the table. His busted eyebrow and lip really did look bad in the LED lighting. "The box in the ground had to be meant for someone other than the man who buried it, right?" he asked. "Why else have nothing but a recording on repeat in there? What would be the point of doing it for yourself?"

"You think he wanted someone else to find it?" Lily couldn't deny she had thought the same before falling asleep the night before. One of many strange possibilities.

"Yeah. I mean, I would have guessed it was some kind of prank had it not been for the man wielding a shovel. That takes a bad joke and turns it into a violent affair. Makes no sense to escalate like that over something supposed to be funny."

Lily took a pull of her coffee. She was seeing the rain and the woods in her memory.

"But then why would he want someone to find the box?" she wondered aloud. "Was it a message? A threat? A weird science experiment?"

"In Kelby Creek? Who knows but here's to hoping he spills his guts when you interrogate him today."

Lily sighed.

"I'm not sure they'll let me talk to him," she admitted. "Other than a statement about being involved, it's not really my place to investigate."

Ant grunted.

"Aren't you a detective? Isn't investigating your whole thing?"

"I am but I was hired for the cold case task force. I don't even report to Detective Lovett on a normal day."

Ant gave her a raised eyebrow again.

"I knew the department was focusing on cold cases but I didn't realize there was a legit task force to do it. I just assumed it was something y'all were doing in your spare time."

It was a common misconception, especially given Dawn County's small size, but Kelby Creek wasn't like most towns. Not since Annie McHale was kidnapped and The Flood followed.

Not since Ida, for some of them at least.

"There were already a few too many cold cases in town before all of the corruption was uncovered," she said diplomatically. "After The Flood everyone wanted to make sure closed, open and dismissed cases alike were handled correctly. Including the people hired to do it. People 'above reproach' and highly motivated. That's why Kenneth Gray got the job of heading it."

"Gray. His wife's murder was a cold case for a long time, wasn't it?"

Lily nodded.

"He was also thoroughly investigated after The Flood and came up as clean as a whistle. He's become somewhat of a symbol for hunting down justice in town now, apparently. We were at lunch after I was first hired and a woman connected to a case he helped close spent the entire meal almost in tears thanking him. He goes the extra mile without being asked, which I like in a boss."

Ant's face was a mask of concentration. He seemed genuinely curious.

"Who else is on the task force?"

"Me and Kathryn Juliet. But she goes by Juliet. Do you know her? She's a few years older. Married to James Hornwell, a nice guy, but didn't take his last name."

Ant shook his head.

"Juliet sounds familiar but, well, I might just be thinking Shakespeare."

Lily hid her smile. Mostly because she'd thought the same thing upon meeting Juliet.

"She's a true local, a few generations deep." Lily sobered. "Her family decided to leave after The Flood but she stayed. Her brother was killed in a car accident in the city shortly after. They were very close. She blames The Flood for his death. She's since been very driven to see that no other traces of corruption go unpunished. She also honestly cares, which is always a good thing."

Neither one of them spoke for a moment. A weight, not unfamiliar, settled between them.

Ant was the one who broke it.

"Then there's you."

Lily took another sip of coffee.

"Then there's me."

The woman stuck in the past.

The woman still hunting for her own justice.

The woman who'd been hollowed out by guilt and anger as a girl.

The woman who had never stopped investigating a case, even as it became as cold as ice over the years.

Lily didn't say any of that, though, and when Ant didn't ask why she'd gotten the job, she knew that *he* knew the answer already.

So instead the silence came back and picked at them.

Lily wanted to do a lot of things to break it—ask him about his life, about his job, about his breakup.

Ask about why he hadn't asked her anything else concerning the lead she'd told him about Ida the night before.

But she didn't.

There were just some wounds too deep and old to ever fully heal.

And, for Lily, one was sitting across the table from her.

ANT COMBED A hand through his hair and hoped Lily Howard couldn't tell he was sitting on a truth he didn't want to be telling.

Her coffee cup was in the sink, his bag was on his back, and they'd made their way to the garage while the rain drizzled on the world around them.

"At least the sun is rising." That was the first thing Lily had said in a few minutes. They'd just been revolving around one another. Normally, he would have spoken up but Ant was trying to tiptoe around his next plans.

He nodded. "I never could decide if rain every day was better than the musty humidity that hung out after. I guess it would be easier just to dislike both, huh?"

Lily flashed a polite smile. Then she glanced at the time on her phone again.

She was anxious to leave.

So was Ant.

"Thanks again for the place to stay," he said, fishing his keys out of his bag. "I like my car but after the all-day drive yesterday it really did feel good to sleep somewhere I actually fit comfortably."

Lily shrugged.

"Thanks for having quick reflexes during the fight. I'm certainly not going to look at a shovel the same way again."

"No problem."

Lily hit the unlock button on her key ring.

"Sorry but I should get going."

Ant held up his hands. He was already backing up.

"I wouldn't want you to miss out on getting that guy to talk."

Lily opened her door but hesitated. Her tone changed when she finally spoke but he couldn't get a beat on the emotion behind it. Maybe it was just plain ol' conversation.

"Are you staying in town or..."

There it was. Time to sidestep the truth.

"For now, yeah. I am."

Then he zipped his mouth shut.

Lily didn't ask for him to elaborate. He could already tell her own wheels were turning for what she had to face at work.

"Good luck."

He waved bye and Lily was fast to go.

It made his next move easier.

Ant pulled out his phone and opened the Google app.

In the search bar he put only one name.

Bryant Lautner.

Chapter Seven

"The man with the shovel is Arturo Hanson. He moved into town a few years back and works at the hardware store downtown. His boss, Mr. Klein, said he's a weird fella but puts in the work and the work's always good."

Kenneth Gray was in a suit wearing a scowl. They were in the hallway outside their office while Juliet was on the phone at her desk. Lily hadn't even put her stuff down before stopping the boss. Not that he seemed to mind.

"I've been around some weird people before and none of them buried boxes with recordings of women screaming in them," Lily pointed out.

Kenneth agreed with that.

"Arturo isn't talking. He *was* cleared by the hospital last night and he's in holding."

Lily was glad for that. In holding meant he was in house, which meant she stood a better chance of getting to him for a conversation.

Kenneth seemed to pick up on that thought. He was nothing but apologetic.

"He lawyered up late last night," he interjected before her hopes could get too high. "That lawyer showed up at the crack of dawn. Arturo might be weird but his lawyer was all straight arrows according to Foster."

Lily held the lid on her emotions tightly closed.

She pushed her shoulders back. She could still feel the strain in her.

"Having a lawyer doesn't preclude me from questioning him, though. And that's what I want to do."

Kenneth was still all apologetic.

"Foster has officially taken the case on, which means you aren't assigned to it." Lily opened her mouth to object, emotions be damned, but Kenneth held up his hand to stop her. "He's agreed to keep us firmly in the loop."

Kenneth flipped his wrist over to look at his watch.

"In fact, we're meeting him in two hours for a full rundown along with the sheriff. Any and all questions, concerns and theories can be shared there. Okay?"

Lily was chomping at the metaphorical bit.

Yet she nodded.

"Okay."

Kenneth motioned to the file tucked under his arm.

"Let's get back to our cold cases and see if we can't heat one of them up until then."

He excused himself while Lily went to her desk. Juliet gave her a quick nod of greeting but never left her phone conversation. Lily did her best to block the woman out to give her some privacy. She booted up her computer, checked her emails when it came to life, and then caught herself staring blankly at the screen.

She didn't like waiting.

In fact, she hated it.

Lily grabbed her phone and went out into the heart of the department before going toward Foster Lovett's office.

The door was open but he wasn't alone inside. Deputy Sterling Costner was standing in front of his desk, his arms motioning to the detective and his voice low. His partner, Marigold Mathers, was leaning against the door in the hallway, arms crossed. She spotted Lily and kept her voice on the low side, too.

"If you want a crack at Foster, you're going to have to wait until Sterling gets it out of his system," Marigold said. "Fair warning, he just started."

Lily wasn't particularly close to anyone at the department but she knew enough about each of her colleagues to form some curiosity and make some light inquiries here and there. However, Sterling Costner's recent brush with danger and his role in bringing down a key player from The Flood, with the help of his now-wife, had been big news that needed no prying to uncover.

But why he was now hot in the face at Foster definitely was a mystery that had her piqued.

"Is this about last night?" Lily asked.

"Yeah." Marigold's expression softened. "He's been beating himself everywhere till Sunday about not finding the hole the first time. Then not staying to wait for you."

"He couldn't have known, on either front."

Marigold sighed so low that if Lily hadn't seen her do it, she wouldn't have known she'd done it at all.

"I know and I'm pretty sure *he* knows but he's still all guilt-ridden. He wants to go back out there and make sure there are no other boxes. He's worried one of them might not just have a recording of a lady screaming but the real thing." Marigold shook her head. "He also really wants to make that Arturo guy talk, but it's not our case, so here we are."

Lily sympathized. "I feel that."

Her plans to try to sway Foster to let her talk to Arturo started to fade fast. She decided to switch gears.

"Speaking about the recording, do you know where it is now?"

"Yeah." Marigold pointed down the hall. "Only because Sterling already demanded to listen to it. It should still be in the meeting room. Sheriff Bennet and Foster were listening to it earlier in there."

Lily backtracked to the meeting room the department used to conduct more convivial interviews. A somewhat new deputy to the department kindly stepped outside the door to give her some privacy.

"A pretty popular recording this morning," he commented before shutting the door behind him.

Lily had no doubt that was true.

The recorder looked odd in the fluorescent lighting. Without rain or mud across it, too. Lily slid into the chair in front of it and ignored the few notes that had been taken on the pad next to it.

If she couldn't talk to Arturo then she could follow up on some other pieces of evidence. Start her own chain of investigation before looping back up to the man in question. After the recording she'd go to the box, and after the box she'd reexamine the scene. Until she was told that there were answers, Lily was going to operate under the assumption that they were still in the questions-only stage.

And she didn't aim to be there long.

Lily put her phone on the table and hit Record. She slipped on some latex gloves and set the tape up to play from the beginning.

The screaming was instant. No wonder Deputy Benz had been quick to shut the door.

"Help!" the woman yelled. *"Help me!"*

Lily leaned forward, head tilting. There was no background sound that she could hear, no ambient noise or even static. It was a clear recording. Just a woman screaming, then, after a minute, the tape noticeably looped.

Lily scanned the notes as the second loop began. According to whoever had jotted down the remarks, the tape in its entirety lasted sixty-two minutes, cutting off during the middle of the last loop. The manufacturer of the recorder had been out of business for ten years, having only found relative success in vintage and novelty equipment before their closing. She took the brand's name, TechTon, and pressed it into her memory as another something to look into once this link in the chain was complete.

"Help! Help me!"

Lily glanced back at the recorder. She let her eyes become unfocused.

A nagging feeling rose in her stomach.

"Help! Help me!"

It clawed its way up through her.

"Help!"

Something…was right there.

"Help me!"

If she could only reach it…

"Help!"

Her adrenaline started to spike. The screams. They sounded familiar…

"Help me!"

But why? Was it from a TV show or movie?

Lily hadn't been an avid watcher of either over the years. She was usually a day late and a buck short when it came to what was trending. She also hadn't lied to Ant about her love life being her professional life. She had as little time for men as she had for Netflix.

But if the scream wasn't recorded from a movie or TV show then how would she know it?

It wasn't Ida's. Her screaming for help was a memory burned forever inside Lily's head. She could pick that sound out of ten bands battling each other for dominance. That sound was a bad laugh track in her nightmares.

Who else's scream would she know?

Who else's scream would she recognize by only a few syllables?

"Help! Help me!"

Lily sat up, ramrod straight.

She clicked the stop button on the recorder and her phone. Her gloves went into the trash on the way out of the meeting room. She was at her desk in less than thirty seconds. The internet search bar was up right after that.

Juliet, now off the phone, turned her attention to her desk mate.

Her dark eyebrows were raised high.

"What's going on, Howie?" There was clear concern

in her question. It wasn't every day that Lily made a
fuss. Even if it was a silent one.

"The recording, the one that we found in the box,"
she started. Lily's fingers were like lightning across the
keyboard. She waited until she found the search results
she was looking for. "I recognized the scream."

Juliet's chair scraped back.

"What do you mean you recognized the scream?"
Lily knew the moment the detective saw her screen.
Juliet let out a little gasp at the video she'd pulled up.
"Are you serious?"

Annie McHale's ransom video was over five years
old but still as captivating as the day it had been up-
loaded by hackers to the town's former website.

Beloved Annie was tied to a chair, hurt and yelling.
It was the only visual anyone had had of her since her
abduction days before it was posted.

Lily put her phone on the desktop. She pressed Play
on her recording.

The second set of screams didn't sync up with Annie's video, but there was no denying they were one
and the same.

"Wow. That's a cruel, weird joke." Juliet huffed.
"But I guess we all knew once Annie's ransom video
went viral there was no avoiding sick ploys for attention like this."

Lily shook her head. Her heartbeat was speeding up
as her thoughts tumbled out ahead of it.

She placed the new nagging feeling easier this time.

"There's static in the video." Lily pressed her finger to the screen so there was no confusion.

"Yeah. There always has been. The FBI tech guys said the video camera wasn't great. Something about its battery. I can't remember."

Lily paused Annie's video but the recording on her phone kept playing.

"The recording has no static. It's as clear as day."

Juliet opened her mouth. Then shut it. They both went back to staring at Lily's phone.

"Maybe it's some new kind of audio trick to filter out the background noise?" Juliet suggested. "They could do that now."

"But why? Why go through that trouble? Why not put the original one in that went viral? Had we not found this version in a buried box, I would have thought it was a sick, easy joke to use her recording."

"But since Annie McHale was never found and *that* was found in a box buried in the woods…"

"What if it was recorded in person?"

Juliet's words were clipped. Analytical. They weren't just talking about some old case. They were talking about *the* case that was the beginning of the end for Kelby Creek. And that held a lot of weight, especially for Juliet. It also was surprisingly heavy for Lily, even though she still resented the attention it had gotten compared to Ida's case.

"You think Arturo was recording Annie McHale in person?"

"Or he might know who did."

Juliet was quiet.

Lily was already onto her next link in the chain.

WHAT ANT LACKED in terms of a badge, he more than made up for in conviction. What he also lacked in polite grace, he compensated for with quick-talking. He knew he might need both when he cut his engine in the parking lot of the Bean Dean Brewery on the north side of town and saw his old friend standing under an umbrella next to her van, a cup of coffee firmly in hand.

The descriptor of "friend" being generous, if he was being honest. The last time Ant had seen Mrs. Jane Dahls, Ida had still been a carefree sixteen-year-old safe and sound at home. Now Mrs. Jane was in her seventies. Though time didn't seem to have wiped away her like for Ant. The moment he was out of the truck, she was calling out to him.

"Mr. Perez, you sure grew another foot since the last time I laid eyes on you."

Ant cracked a smile and met the woman with a careful embrace. His former babysitter did indeed seem to be smaller than he remembered.

"I kept growing to make sure I could reach every high shelf in the grocery store that you ever needed me to reach," he returned. "Don't think I forgot about that time that I had to climb up on the shelf to grab you some wafers and almost took out the entire aisle when I fell."

Mrs. Jane was rolling her eyes when he stepped back but she was still smiling.

"I never asked you to become a monkey and scale up the thing. That was all you and those young-boy urges to climb everything." She chuckled. "Though I'll say I'll never forgot how Robert Tate Sr. nearly had a heart attack when the whole thing started wobbling. Like one shelf of cookies falling was going to bankrupt him. God rest his overdramatic soul."

Ant nodded, though he'd forgotten about the owner of the grocery store nearly losing his head over it all.

Then again, he'd forgotten a lot about his past.

There wasn't much use in remembering it. Most times it just hurt.

Which was why he'd called Mrs. Jane after all these years for a meeting.

Not only was she whip smart, she was a front-porch vigilante. She had long-standing knowledge of the town and most of its locals thanks to her skills in the art of word-of-mouth information and her being tapped into the gossip mill since the '80s.

She knew things.

She knew people.

Now Mrs. Jane proved that herself. She gave Ant a long look. Her smile folded.

"I heard about the woods last night," she said. "Must have been hard to be out there, especially with Miss Howard. How's she doing?"

Ant didn't ask how she knew about the night before—all it took was one deputy to mention it to a loved one, who then mentioned it to someone else, and eventually that someone went to Mrs. Jane—but he kept his answer vague regardless.

"She's good. Held her own. She's at work now."

Mrs. Jane nodded deep. She reached her free hand out and touched his arm.

"And what about you? How are you doing?" Her gaze went to his eyebrow, then lip. He was surprised she hadn't lead with the question.

Ant took her hand in his and squeezed before letting it go.

"Nothing I can't handle."

Mrs. Jane had never been one to leave something like that without prodding but this time she did.

"I bet," she said instead. "Is that why you called on me? The man in the woods?"

Ant shook his head.

"No, ma'am. I actually wanted to ask you about someone else. The guy I'm trying to find is named Bryant Lautner. Have you heard of him?"

Mrs. Jane chewed on that for a little bit.

She nodded, slow.

"I haven't heard the name in a while but yes. After what happened to his wife, poor man has had a whole slew of problems through the years."

Ant could feel his blood pumping harder.

"Has had?" Ant repeated. "Meaning he's still around here?"

"I mean, I haven't seen him since he moved out of his and his late wife's house, but I think he's still rattling around that workshop of his."

That had Ant's ears up.

"He has a workshop?"

Mrs. Jane snorted, rolling her eyes one more time.

"Him and his little golfing buddies used to joke that

it was a way to escape their wives and have a few beers without being nagged. Once Patricia passed, the joke wasn't funny anymore. If you ask me, it never was."

"But you said he doesn't live there anymore?"

"He doesn't live at his old house but the workshop wasn't on that property. I actually don't know who owns the land it's on. I always assumed it belonged to his father."

"But you know where it is?"

Mrs. Jane looked peachy proud.

"Buy me a muffin and I'll write down the directions."

Ant didn't hesitate.

"Yes, ma'am."

Chapter Eight

Foster got a call from his wife, Millie, and was off before Lily could tell him what she thought she'd discovered. Kenneth, however, lapped up the news. He had Annie McHale's video up on the computer in the cold case task force's office and was paying rapt attention.

"I can't believe I didn't get this earlier," he said, after pausing the video and playing the recording twice. "This is a great catch, Lily."

Lily was standing next to Juliet, who seconded the sentiment.

"Especially since poor Annie yelling for help used to be a soundtrack to this town." Juliet's expression turned in on itself, propelled by grief. If Annie McHale had never been kidnapped, Juliet's brother never would have died in the city after leaving town.

It was a sore spot.

That sore spot was also what made Juliet a great detective. Just like Kenneth's late wife's murder and his pursuit of justice made him a more driven man now.

That said, Lily didn't fault either of them for missing the connection.

The only reason Lily had recognized Annie's screams was because she, at first, knew without a doubt that they hadn't been Ida's.

"I'd like to talk to him now," Lily said, sidestepping their praise. "Arturo."

Kenneth rubbed his jaw in thought.

It wasn't a thought that was going to give her a way into the investigation she'd already been side-lined from.

"If this recording is authentic, then that means Arturo either recorded Annie during her captivity in person or he knew someone who did," Kenneth underlined. "That's insanely big news. Which means we need to make sure we handle it right." He pushed back in the chair. "I need to talk to Foster and the sheriff first."

If Lily were one to show outbursts of emotion, she would have made a growling noise. Instead she shifted her hip, putting her more squarely between her boss and the door.

"Annie was five years ago," Lily said. "That box buried in the ground was yesterday. What if there are other boxes? What if one of them has an actual woman inside it?"

She could see Kenneth consider that.

She could also see he understood her frustration.

"Arturo lawyered up and, quite frankly, putting the person who helped knock him out the night before in front of him isn't going to help anyone. But let me talk to Foster. The reason this task force works is because we have clear boundaries for our cases and for current cases."

Lily nodded. She didn't grit her teeth until he was out in the hallway and out of earshot.

Juliet waited.

"He's right, you know," she said. "But just because you can't talk to Arturo right now doesn't mean you can't work him. Right?"

The adrenaline rush of finding a lead refueled and redirected.

"You're right."

Lily was back at her computer and searching again. Juliet went to her desk and did the same. If Arturo had an original recording of Annie, then there had to be a connection between them somehow.

Somewhere.

Lily did a deep dive on the internet, scouring any and all public information on Arturo. She came up with four poorly made social media profiles. Two were public; only one had been used in the past year. Several posts complained of the weather, local politics and income tax. One was a rant about what a load of crock mechanics were based on how much they charged to fix problems he could do himself. That post had a picture attached of an old Ford without its tires. The vehicle was up on four cinder blocks.

Lily saved the picture before reexamining it.

The truck was beneath a metal overhang sitting above a cracked concrete slab. That slab was at the end of what looked like a dirt road. Grass and more dirt could be seen around it. In the background there were trees, thick and green.

Lily went back to the date on the original post.

A year and some months ago.

The location tag was off but when it came to the woods, Lily was an expert.

She scoured the rest of his public profiles and found two more pictures of the same overhang and carport. One was the same setup but the other picture was angled from the side. In it she could see the building it was attached to. It was a narrow wooden structure that was as worn as the brush around it was overgrown.

There was also a sign in the distance. More worn and weathered than the building.

"No Fishing" could just barely be made out across its front.

Directly behind it was what looked like another dirt road.

Lily took a moment and closed her eyes.

When she opened them again, she knew where she needed to go.

MRS. JANE HAD a muffin and twenty minutes later, Ant was staring at Bryant Lautner's workshop.

After leaving the café Ant had been pure speed. Every mile he ate up, every turn he whipped around and every tree he passed he felt a surge of purpose. Of energy. Of dogged hope that he was going to cinch an answer.

Finally.

Now, though, that feeling was deflating.

The workshop looked like it hadn't been touched in years.

Ant crept up to the front door, minding the windows

on either side. He'd already parked his car further back
in the trees and made his way up the road quickly and
quietly. Thin lead or not, he wasn't taking any chances
of spooking the one man he needed to question.

If it had been anyone else—if he had been there for
anything else—Ant might have questioned his methods.

But it was for Ida. This could *be* Ida's abductor.

Ant felt the heat of rage rise within him. He shook his
shoulders out to belay it. The first window was blocked
by a curtain. The second, something wooden. He went
to the door last. He knocked harder than he'd meant
to knock.

Ant waited for movement but nothing happened. No
back doors or windows opening and shutting, no one
running off into the woods to hide from him.

No nothing.

Ant gave it another series of loud knocks.

No sounds inside. None outside, either. Only birds
singing, probably happy that the rain had let up.

Ant stood there a moment.

He should leave—there obviously hadn't been someone there in a while—but he couldn't.

It was quiet but it was there. In the back of his mind.

Ida, yelling for him.

Ant sighed heavy and true.

He wasn't leaving until he'd seen the inside.

Like Mrs. Jane had described it, the building was
on the smaller side. Without going in, Ant pictured
one open living area, a bathroom, and maybe a sepa-
rate room that acted as a bedroom or storage. The back

porch had seen better days but held firm beneath his weight as he tried the back door. It didn't budge an inch.

Ant tried the windows next. One was painted shut, the other was flimsy as all get-out. He pushed on the latter until it slid all the way up. Once again, no one moved or made a sound.

So he climbed in.

If the outside hadn't been well kept, Ant would have known just by the smell inside that the workshop had been left closed up for a long while. It was stale air mixed with a dampness that pressed against him when he straightened.

The main room was more or less like he'd pictured it. Open but missing most of the furniture. There was a small kitchenette in the corner and a lone patio couch next to the front door. But to his surprise there were three doors that led off the main room. He unlocked the back door, just in case he needed to get out quick if someone came in through the front, before he went to the first one.

Ant didn't knock this time. The door opened with no problem.

A billiard table took up most of the space. It would have been out of place had it not matched the run-down vibe of the rest of the workshop. The whole thing was leaning to one corner, sloped and stained. The green felt was torn and the legs beneath were struggling to stay upright. Ant wasn't sure but he didn't think disuse alone could have put the table in such bad shape. A fight could have done the trick; so could horsing around. If Bryant and his buddies had used the workshop as an escape from their wives then there probably was a drunken mix of the two at some point.

Ant went to the second room next.

The bathroom was small and surprisingly not as dingy. It also had running water. He flipped the light switch. The lights struggled on.

Ant looked up at them, curious.

So the workshop hadn't been completely abandoned.

Ant started to go for the third door but froze at the sound of footsteps. Someone was walking up the back steps.

Ant moved inside the billiard room and grabbed a cobweb-covered pool cue off the wall in one fluid movement. He kept it low at his side, ready. He usually wasn't a man to hide but he didn't want to startle Bryant Lautner into running or shooting, if he was like most Southern property owners and carried a gun.

Ant held his breath as the back door creaked open, slow. He shouldn't have unlocked it. Now Bryant was going to know someone was inside. Ant put himself in a better stance to fight, if needed. Or run, if he decided that was the better option.

It was a mistake.

He hit a spot on the floor that creaked louder than the back door had.

Ant cussed low. There was no point pretending he wasn't there now.

"I'm just here to talk," he decided to yell out. "I'm coming out, unarmed."

He put the stick on the table, brought his hands up

and entered the main room, hoping to God that Bryant Lautner didn't shoot first, ask questions later.

All his hope and he still got a gun pointed at him.

All his luck made the person aiming it a sight for sore eyes.

Lily's eyebrows were sky high. She lowered her gun.

"You're still following me?" she exclaimed. "How do you think that's a good idea?"

Ant dropped his hands.

"Following you?" He closed the gap between them. "I'm not following you."

She didn't look convinced.

"Then why are you here?"

Ant thought it was obvious. He said as much.

"The same reason you are. Bryant Lautner."

If her initial surprise at seeing him could be scaled at a ten out of ten, the look that scrunched her face now ranked at a solid thirteen.

"You aren't here because of Bryant?" he followed up.

She shook her head. "No."

Lily's body language changed for the worse. It put him even closer to the edge.

"Then why?" he asked, low.

Lily opened her mouth but no words came out.

A car door shut out front.

Both Ant's and Lily's heads turned in sync.

"Were you expecting anyone?" Ant asked.

Lily pulled up her gun. It was enough of an answer, but still she added to it.

"I wasn't even expecting you."

Chapter Nine

Lily had Ant's hand and was pulling him out the back door in a move that was the epitome of clumsy stealth. It only came after the decision that getting caught inside of a suspect's house alone, without permission, wasn't a smart move. Getting caught inside a suspect's house *with* a civilian was even less appealing.

So Ant's hand was warm in hers as the two made it out of the door and into the trees surrounding the building. He, thankfully, understood her intent. He was quiet and quick. They made it into the cover of the trees before the sound of the front door shutting echoed out to them.

Lily holstered her gun and peeked around a tree at the building.

No one was looking back. Nor were they yelling.

"I don't think anyone saw us," she breathed out. Her shoulders dragged down a little. She'd been sloppy. She wasn't happy about it.

Ant was taking cover behind a neighboring tree.

"Won't he see your car?" he asked.

"No. I parked off the main road. I'm not exactly supposed to be here."

Ant faced her. A whisper of a smirk was across his lips.

"Great minds," he said, simply. "Mine is off a ways, too. I didn't want Bryant to get spooked."

"Bryant?" Lily looked away from the house completely, shifting her attention to Ant. She didn't understand. "Bryant Lautner?"

Ant stepped back so he was securely behind the tree.

"Yeah. This was his workshop back in the day. Word was he still hangs out here." That was news to Lily. "But you're not here because of Bryant...or me?"

Lily shook her head.

"I'm here for Arturo Hanson."

They clearly weren't on the same page.

"Who's Arturo Hanson?" he asked.

"The guy with the shovel who attacked us. I found some old social media posts he made with pictures that looked like they were taken here. So I thought I'd come check the place out."

"And you didn't knock?"

Lily felt a brief flair of professional shame. She shook it off in the next second.

"There wasn't a vehicle, no lights, and I wasn't looking to be surprised. Then I saw the open window and tried the back door. And, well, then *you*." She waved her hand through the air to stop the conversation. "But we can talk about all of this later. Right now we need to go see who showed up and ask them some questions."

Ant looked skeptical. He craned his neck around the tree to see the house again. He nodded to the right.

"We can go that way, curve around and walk up to the front door. Might feel a bit hinky since neither one of us is rolling up in a car, though, but maybe that badge of yours will distract them from asking about our transportation."

He wasn't wrong. Lily used her free hand to confirm her badge was hanging on the chain outside her blazer.

"Listen, I don't want to break eye contact with this place, even for a second," she said. "If this really is Bryant's place, then this is a lead. If it's not, it's still a lead for Arturo. I'm not letting whoever just showed up get away without identifying them and asking some questions. Got it?"

Ant sense of urgency seemed to mirror hers.

"Let's hurry then."

They circled the building and kept to the trees. No one came out, no one yelled. Lily only took a small beat when they were near the front before hustling toward the front porch. She paused one more time by the car to confirm that no one was inside.

"It's running," she realized, whispering over her shoulder to Ant. "Whoever is here, they're not planning on staying long."

It was an old Cadillac and not at all in good condition. White paint chipped, everything silver rusted to some degree, and the interior wasn't faring any better. There was nothing notable in view on the seats. A quick look showed no plates. Ant beat Lily to taking a quick picture with his phone. Lily beat him to the front porch steps.

Something Ant wasn't too keen on.

He shouldered in front of Lily before she could make it to the door.

"I'm the one with the gun and badge," she whispered quickly.

Ant leaned over, eyes still on the door, and matched her volume. He was so close she could feel his breath on her cheek.

"A badge and gun don't mean a thing if someone starts shooting."

Lily was about to point out that it meant she'd start shooting back but he had his knuckles up ready to knock.

"Dawn County Sheriff's Department," she called out, beating him to the punch. "We just want to talk!"

No response.

Ant turned his head a little like Cook did when he was trying to suss out a sound. He shook his head. Lily knocked and repeated her call again.

They waited.

Not one sound.

Ant was tensing up by the second. He put his ear to the door and then shook his head again.

"Nothing," he mouthed.

Lily pulled her gun out of its holster. She kept it at her side.

"We could go around back again," Ant offered. "We know the door is open."

Lily didn't like that idea.

Just like she wasn't a fan of the new feeling in her gut.

Something wasn't right.

Just like a woman's voice screaming from beneath the ground.

Just like that rising, burning feeling she'd felt in the woods while chasing an unknown man dragging off a girl into the dark.

Urgency, deep and powerful, came next.

True urgency.

Lily glanced at Ant. He looked so much like he had that night. Dark hair wet with creek water and rain, a hardened face trying to figure out why the world wasn't lining up the way it was supposed to, eyes as black as the night his sister was disappearing into.

Lily put her hand on the doorknob and turned. It was unlocked. They didn't have the time to wait.

The door opened with ease.

Whatever happened next, she and Ant were in it together.

THE LIGHTS WEREN'T ON.

It was the second thing Ant noticed as he and Lily went inside.

The first?

No one was home.

At least not in the main room.

Lily had her service weapon at the ready. Ant had his fists balled.

"Dawn County Sheriff's Department," she yelled out. Still nothing.

The back door was still unlocked. The window he'd climbed through was still open. The same went for the door to the bathroom that was ajar, the light on inside.

Ant nudged Lily and nodded to the pool table room.

She took the lead with notable aggression.

Ant hurried in after her.

Nothing had changed and no one else was waiting for them there.

Lily backed out. Ant grabbed the pool cue he'd wielded earlier and followed.

It might not be a gun but he could still make it hurt if he needed.

There was only one room left that neither had seen inside before. Ant did a dance around her to get to the doorknob first. Lily raised her gun. She didn't need to say a word to let him know this was it.

This was game time and she wasn't going to be the one to fumble the ball.

The second Ant had the door open, Lily took a powerful step forward.

Then she stopped as if she'd hit a brick wall.

Ant was behind her in a flash.

He was so dumbstruck he couldn't even find the right cuss to fit the situation.

The room was the same size as the one with the pool table, and just as decrepit. The paint was escaping parts of the wall, the floor had chips in it and there was a slight sag in the roof. Still it was in far better shape than what was stored within it.

The trash alone would have been alarming. There were bags and wrappers among bottles and beakers and plastic containers cluttering the floor. Batteries sat on top of a pail of kitty litter in the corner, a blender beaten to near death on a table next to it. Buckets and paper towels and rubbing alcohol containers were scattered around like clunky confetti. Ant stopped next to a spool of aluminum foil and a pile of coffee filters. Lily was slightly ahead of him, stopping again by several strainers, rubber tubing and a propane cylinder on its side. Beneath the window opposite them was a twin mattress, stripped bare, on the floor. A lone pillow without a case was at its head.

Lily lowered her gun. She covered her nose with her arm and turned to him.

"Back out of here," she said on a hurried breath. "This is a meth lab."

It should have clicked sooner but the moment she said it, everything in the room made sense.

Everything but an open box at the foot of the mattress. There was something at the very top. Something that didn't fit the rest of the room but something they'd definitely seen before.

Ant pointed to it, covering his nose and mouth with his other arm in an attempt to avoid exposure to the hazardous chemicals around them.

"One of these things is not like the other."

Lily was fast. Her gun went into her holster and she pulled a pair of blue latex gloves out of her blazer pocket. She was on the box in seconds, picking up the item on top.

"It's a recorder." Lily turned the black box this way and that between her hands. "It's identical to the one that was buried."

Ant, who had up until then thought of the workshop as something only related to Bryant Lautner, said the obvious.

"This all can't be a coincidence."

Lily didn't comment on the thought. She was peering into the box.

"This thing is filled with recorders. Maybe ten. Maybe twelve." Lily's gaze went back to the one in her hand.

"Does that one have a tape in it?" Ant asked her.

Lily answered by clicking the play button.

The screaming that echoed out of it wasn't as off-putting as it had been the night before, but that didn't mean Ant was a fan. He watched Lily visibly tense.

"It's Annie McHale again."

Ant had to pause at that.

He had sympathy for what had happened to Annie, but that didn't stop the well of resentment that lived within him at her family. At Kelby Creek. It was why he avoided talking about Annie and The Flood in general. Others could shake their heads and say *what a pity.* Ant had a harder time not comparing everything to Ida.

"What do you mean it's Annie again?" There was no point sugarcoating his voice. It was dripping in his feelings that he knew, in some small part, Lily shared.

Lily was unfazed. Her attention went back to the box. Where it went after that, Ant wouldn't know.

A car door shut outside.

Ant didn't wait around to see what happened next.

He was out of the room and on the front porch in a blink. The mention of Annie, the possibility that Bryant Lautner was connected to Ida, and Lily showing up for the man that had nearly maimed her all had Ant raring to go.

The Cadillac reversing at an alarming speed was just the cherry on top that he needed.

"Hey!"

Ant jumped off the porch in one quick bound. The distance between him and the car was widening. He couldn't see who was driving.

"Stop!"

The car gave off a God-awful squeal. The driver swung it around so both were facing the dirt road. Ant wasn't going to stand for that. He charged ahead with every intention of catching the car when the driver had to slow down to turn. Then he could open the door and get some answers. At the very least he could get a better look at the driver's face.

It didn't take long to realize that he was actually going to do it. He could catch it. He was fast enough.

He—

He smelled smoke.

And it wasn't coming from the car.

Ant stopped in his tracks. Ice filled his veins. He spun around, abandoning his pursuit of the car and hoping with all his might that Lily had followed him out of the house. That she was sprinting only a few steps behind him.

But she wasn't.

All he saw were the budding flames that were now licking the right side of the workshop.

"Lily!"

The car behind him kicked up dirt and rocks. It became background noise to him repeating Lily's name.

Those were the last two things he heard before the workshop exploded.

Chapter Ten

The heat.

Blistering as it was, it didn't compare to the force of the explosion.

Ant went from upright and facing the house to on his back staring up at the sky within the blink of an eye. Pain was a burn in his chest; pressure was a vise on his lungs. He was coughing before he was sitting up and was pretty damn sure that something on him was broken. Cracked at the least. Bruised for certain.

Ant wasn't going to know for a while because there was no way he was going to sit there, take a break and tally up his injuries. Not when he had no idea where Lily was. He rolled onto his side and managed to push up. It took him two tries but he made it up with a wobble. He coughed all the while, trying to suck in the air that had been knocked out of him. Enough, at least, to yell.

"Lily!"

The house was a scene right out of a nightmare. Flames ate at the entire right side of the building, dark smoke rolling up high, while the left side looked like it had been simultaneously crushed and then snapped like a rubber band stretched out too far. The porch was crippled and the front door was broken in two. None of it stopped Ant. He covered his nose and mouth with an aching arm and ventured inside what used to be a building.

"Lily!"

Ant kicked away broken remnants of the structure around him, only eyeing the buckling ceiling above the living space with mild concern for himself. He made it two steps toward where the second bedroom had been before he had to stop. There was no way he was getting inside that room.

It wasn't even a room anymore.

That ice in his veins hardened into a weight that threatened to drag him all the way down.

If Lily had been in that room when it blew…

No.

He wasn't going to accept that.

Ant pulled his shirt up to his nose and surveyed the destruction in front of him. There wasn't any way he could get into the area safely. In fact, he doubted there was a way he could break through the debris without bringing down the rest of the building. But maybe if he was fast… Maybe if he dove in with his fists and muscle he could dig her out… Maybe if—

Coughing.

It was faint but it was unmistakable.

Ant spun to his left, trying to track the sound.

"Lily?"

Something shifted near the back door. It was a part

of the ceiling, now on the floor. The boot that moved beneath it was like a gut punch.

"Lily," he yelled. "I'm here!"

Ant made it over and tossed the wood to the side just in time to see Lily struggling to push herself off the floor. She was on her stomach, with her weight spread between it and her elbows. The effort didn't seem to be working. At least not fast enough.

A loud cracking noise split through the flames lapping up the beams.

Ant couldn't be gentle, but he could be fast.

He moved his arm beneath Lily's waist and pulled her up against him. She started to convulse in a coughing fit. Ant felt for her but he wasn't about to stop and hang around. Holding her close, Ant ran out of the building and into the woods. He didn't even think about slowing until the trees enveloped them.

When he finally did, he still didn't let Lily go completely.

"I got you," he told her. He crouched down and tried to maneuver her onto her back with as little jostling as possible.

Good intentions but bad execution. He lost his balance and fell to the dirt with a painful thud. Lily slipped out of his hold but he was quick to wrangle her against him so she didn't hit the ground.

Her long hair, smelling of smoke, rested against his chest. Her coughing became a slow reverberation that went all the way through him. Ant kept one arm wrapped firmly around her, as if it was a safety measure against the danger that had exploded around them.

If Lily minded, she didn't say so.

Once she caught her breath, he felt her relax into him a bit.

They sat like that for a few moments before the cracking sound grew sharper, louder, echoing through the trees.

Bryant Lautner's workshop seemed to take one big collective breath before collapsing in on itself.

Ant couldn't move. He could only watch the way the smoke became darker, reaching for the sky above them like a hand of death.

A hand that had almost taken Lily.

Ant tightened his hold ever so slightly on the woman against him.

THE FIRE DEPARTMENT couldn't save the building by the time they arrived fifteen minutes later so they focused on saving the trees instead. An ambulance hauled tail between Sheriff Bennet's truck and Detective Gray's shiny new SUV. Two deputy cruisers rounded out the caravan but Lily was sure others were spread out and blocking the road off at both ends.

The rest of the department sure as hell better be trying to find the man in the Cadillac.

"Detective Howard, I'm telling you we're going to the hospital," the EMT named Colton said after a cursory examination at the road.

Lily had one leg out of the ambulance and the other ready to walk her the rest of the way out of the back. Her attention was past them to the sheriff. Blake Bennet was huffing and puffing on her cell phone and her radio, pacing a line in the dirt. Her braid was swinging, her lips thin and angry.

"And I'm telling you I feel fine," Lily shot back at the man. She motioned to her body. It probably wasn't the most convincing move. She hadn't caught her reflection yet but by the concern in everyone's eyes, she wasn't winning any awards for being pristine.

Movement from the side of the ambulance drew her attention. Ant had his arms crossed over his chest. He eyed her like she was an errant child.

"You just got blown up by a meth lab." His words were stern, matching his body language. "And before you try to downplay that just remember that I'm the one who helped lift a piece of the ceiling off you. You're going to the hospital."

Lily was shocked at the resolve. Though not as much as she had been at the situation they'd wound up in. She'd come chasing a thin lead. She was about to leave in an ambulance.

It didn't sit right with her.

"The bulk of the explosion was in the other room and we weren't exposed long," she tried.

Ant and the EMT weren't having it. They spit some more concern and facts her way until Sheriff Bennet's gaze swung to Lily's and everything turned angry. She moved her phone to her shoulder and hollered.

"Why aren't y'all on the way to Haven? Get going!"

Lily didn't want to be toted off to the hospital. She wanted to stay and work the scene, or dig deep on the clues she'd found inside, but the sheriff's words stopped her short.

The sheriff hadn't held her position long but she was no stranger to the power of her command.

EMT Colton she could bypass. Ant she could maybe sway. Sheriff Bennet's orders? She didn't want to push her luck.

"Fine." Lily pulled her legs back in. "But I'm telling you, I'm okay."

No sooner had she said it than she was struck by breath-stealing pain as she attempted to settle on the gurney. Lily gathered up every acting skill she had to hide the pain.

It didn't work.

Ant got in behind her and sat on the bench at her side.

"Next time you say that, hide the flinch and I might believe you."

Colton banged on the window to the front seat to signal the driver. He told the man to take it slow on the pits and dips of the aged road.

"We about lost an axle flooring it here," he explained to them. "Though I guess it was worth the risk to avoid getting stuck in the mud had it been flooding again." He made a tsking sound. "My cousin Benny is a firefighter in the county over and said they had to call in the cavalry after one of their trucks got sucked into a ditch last night. We only have the two ambulances in Dawn County so I think we better not chance it breaking down."

Lily wasn't going to comment, mainly because she didn't think it was a conversation worth having. Small talk wasn't her favorite thing, especially coupled with being in a tight space. Ant, though, seemed to really take to it.

"I worked on towing a fire truck once back at my last job working for a mechanic," he told Colton. "It was tricky business. My boss about blew a gasket after our first towing line snapped."

Lily tilted her head a little at that.

"I didn't know you worked as a mechanic. The last I heard you were tending bar in Richmond."

Ant laughed.

"The last you heard was a few years ago. It's been a hot minute since I was slinging drinks in Virginia."

A tinge of *something* pinched at Lily.

No one had expected her to keep in touch with Ant through the years and she hadn't. Only a few times had it been necessary to track him down to speak about Ida's case. She already knew her knowledge of his life as an adult was slim. Yet there she was, feeling a certain way about it.

"I wasn't much a fan of bartending, to tell you the truth," he told Colton. "I know you must see some holy horrible things at this job but when I say I saw my fair share of bloodshed and cringe-worthy injuries while doling out alcohol, let me tell you I mean it."

Colton didn't challenge Ant's claim and the conversation took another turn toward convivial. Lily didn't pretend to want to join. She instead turned inward to catalog how she was feeling. It wasn't until they took a turn into the parking lot of Haven Hospital that Lily finally circled in on what was bothering her.

The realization must not have been missed. While Colton spoke to the driver, Ant leaned in.

"If you won't tell the professional what's hurting, tell me, so I can do absolutely nothing helpful since I know more about cars and beer than humans."

His sarcasm barely concealed his concern. Lily rolled her eyes but kept the same closeness between them.

"It's not what's hurting," she said. "It's what's not sitting right with me."

"And what's that? Because, I'll be honest, none of what's happened since I got back to Kelby Creek has been sitting right with me."

Lily shook her head. It hurt.

She kept on.

"Let's make an assumption that whoever started the fire knew exactly where they were starting it. That they knew a meth lab filled with hazardous materials was right there, just waiting for a spark."

"An easy assumption to make," Ant added.

"And, since you told me the only person you told was Mrs. Jane and until Juliet asks if she told anyone we're going to act like she didn't, we didn't tell anyone when and where we were going, let's assume that no one knew we were out there." She didn't mention the fact that she and Ant had both hidden their cars from view, though that was definitely a point in the No One Knew They Were There column.

"All right."

"That means someone meant to destroy that house and they meant to do it while it was empty. Why?"

Ant's brow furrowed. This close to him, Lily let her

eyes trace his face, follow the smears of dirt and sweat across his skin. She felt relief at the distance he'd managed to put between the workshop and himself before the explosion. It had been his yell for her that had made her drop the recorder and bolt from the room. Had she not tripped, she would have made it out of the building safely and not needed this trip to the hospital.

"Well, from what I heard you tell Detective Gray, it was a textbook meth lab in there," Ant supplied. "Maybe a competitor wanted to end its production? Maybe it was Bryant's *or* Arturo's and they wanted someone to cover it up?"

Lily snapped her fingers.

"That's another thing." She lowered her voice even more. "It was textbook. Yet the rest of the house didn't smell like anything other than mildew. Why was there no spillover into the rest of the house?"

Lily quieted as the ambulance came to a stop. The EMT opened the back doors and hopped out. He was waving at someone inside the hospital.

Ant's attention was still squarely on Lily.

"You don't think it was real. The meth lab."

Lily shrugged through her pain.

"The recorders are the only thing in that house that made sense to me. They connect us back to the box in the ground and Arturo, both of which sent me there in the first place." Colton was talking to a nurse who'd come out. Lily side-eyed them to make sure they weren't listening. Ant came in so close that Lily could feel his warmth against her cheek. "If we can't get answers from the box, that workshop, or Arturo, then maybe the re-cording itself is where we look now."

"Annie McHale screaming." He sucked on his teeth a second. "That's a case worked to death. Are you look-ing to ask the FBI agents who investigated or go local? Because you and I both know neither are going to give you much. I'm sure they've lost count of how many tips, leads and conspiracy theories they've gotten over the years."

Lily knew that was true.

She also knew something Ant didn't.

"Not every McHale left town after the investigation was over. I know someone who stayed."

Chapter Eleven

Any and all investigative routes Lily had been itching to take were blocked by the simple fact that she was worse off than she'd pretended to be.

Where her ribs weren't bruised, they were broken. She had a concussion that brought on a headache that had made her sick. There was a nasty cut along the back of her thigh from falling debris and bruising along the front of her from being thrown to the ground.

By the time she got into an examination room at the hospital she'd gone from telling everyone she was fine to asking for pain meds.

Ant didn't like it. He didn't like it at all.

When the doctor insisted she get into a hospital gown and right into a bed, he was a mass of constantly moving anxiousness. He hovered, he insisted, he was eventually told to leave. He would, though only after she spoke to him, before the meds took over.

"They want me to stay the night but I don't have anyone to watch Cook," Lily told him when they finally were alone. Ant could tell she was trying not to move too much. The sight ate at him.

"I can see to him," he said. "We already know he's a fan of me."

Lily gave him a brief smile. She let her head rest back against the pillow. Ant didn't want to get too close, even though he'd changed out of his contaminated clothing into scrubs the hospital had given him.

Yet it was a hard personal ask. Every time he looked at her, he wanted to do the opposite.

He wanted to hold her again like he'd done in the woods.

He wanted to protect her.

"Juliet is going out there to get a file from my office," Lily added, becoming more quiet on every syllable. "She won't mind giving you a ride."

"I'll make sure everything is good," he promised, forgoing reaching for her hand. "Don't you worry."

Lily's eyes closed but Ant stayed a moment longer.

She'd been blown up the day after she'd been attacked.

Leaving her didn't feel right.

The rhythmic beep of the monitor next to the bed was steady.

Lily was okay for now.

But he'd thought she was okay that morning when he'd left.

A nurse came in then and shooed him into the hall with reassurances that Lily just needed to rest. Once he stepped out, Detective Juliet approached him. She'd obviously heard the nurse's comment.

"I'd sleep for a week straight after all of that, truth

be told." She eyed him critically. "I don't know how you're not laid up, too."

Ant shrugged off the concern.

"She took the brunt of it, believe me. All I needed was an ibuprofen."

"Tough guy." She grinned. "No wonder Howie's been hanging with you."

The detective told him to call her Juliet and, as Lily had said, had no issue with letting him tag along to her house. Their conversation on the ride over was surprisingly bland, though. Ant wasn't sure why she wasn't bringing up the workshop, Lautner or Arturo, but he wasn't going to be the one to do so.

If he was being honest, the idea of discussing the case with a woman who wasn't Lily felt wrong somehow.

He did, however, decide that he liked Juliet. She was easygoing until it was time to focus. The second they walked into Lily's house she met Cook with a whole heap of scratches before making a game plan.

"I'll meet you here when I'm done. It shouldn't be long. Well, unless she doesn't have any sort of ordering system to her files then I might be a bit." She sighed but it didn't feel accusatory. "Bless her, Howie's good, but sometimes she's too good."

Ant liked the compliment. He wasn't sure Lily would. Neither was he sure about the nickname.

"I've heard her called a lot of things but I don't think I've heard Howie."

Juliet laughed freely. She pointed at Cook, still bouncing between them.

"I'm a firm believer that Cook and Howie has a great *Turner & Hooch* ring to it." She spread her hands out in the air between them like she was reading a banner. She adopted an announcer-style voice. "Cook and Howie, service dog and dogged detective fighting injustice while trying to navigate the small town niceties… that and Mrs. Belview's constant complaints about the neighborhood kids walking on her grass."

She was grinning. It was definitely a bit she'd done before. She looked at him for a reaction but his focus had shifted.

"I didn't realize Cook was a service dog with the department." Cook nudged his hand, picking up on his name. "I guess that's why he held his own in a fight."

"Oh, no, I *wish* he was with our department. I've been told Kelby Creek is looking to build us a K-9 unit next but I've been holding my breath with that news for two years." The next part came out so effortlessly that Ant guessed Juliet probably hadn't even realized she was sharing it. Or had assumed that Ant was a lot closer with Lily than he was. "Cook was a PTSD service dog in North Carolina. Lily got him just as the funding to the program was cut. She petitioned to keep him and now he's the adorable leading man in the duo that is Cook and Howie." Juliet swooped her hand down to give the dog a few more pets.

Then all the jovial easiness from the detective became focused. Before Ant could collect his thoughts, she was clouding them up again.

"I know she was concerned about him for the night

but did she ask you to pack a bag for her? If she's staying at the hospital, she'll probably need one."

Lily hadn't asked. She hadn't asked for anything for herself since they'd arrived at Haven Hospital. Her concern had landed on him and Cook only.

"Yeah, she did," he lied. "I'm running up there now."

Juliet led the way until they went in opposite directions at the top of the stairs. Cook followed Ant and looked up at him once they were both inside the bedroom.

"PTSD, huh?" Ant patted the dog's head. "I didn't realize she was having issues."

The second he whispered it to Cook, Ant felt shame wallop him.

He was the brother who'd lost his sister. He'd been attacked, left for dead and then left searching for years. Ant didn't settle. He didn't form long-standing relationships. He didn't even stay in the same place for more than six months.

He had trauma.

He had nightmares.

He hadn't thought about Lily in the same light.

She had drive, determination and a career she'd been cultivating since leaving town. Sure, Ant knew there had to be scars there. Emotional, mental.

Yet, there he was in her bedroom, for the first time realizing he hadn't wondered about Lily's suffering.

He was the brother who had lost his sister. She was the girl who had run into the darkness ahead of him.

He'd been attacked. She'd fought, too.

He'd been left for dead in the creek water. She'd been the one to pull him out.

He'd been the one screaming out for Ida in the rain. She'd been the one that spent years in law enforcement…only to come right back with training, skills and a life that had been forever changed by a night in the woods.

Of course, she wouldn't have just gotten over that.

Who would?

Who could?

Ant wanted to talk to Lily, right then and there, and apologize.

He was sorry he hadn't kept in touch. He was sorry he hadn't been there for her. He was sorry that, even now, she might be in the same boat as him.

Lily Howard might have spent the past fourteen years seeing the same ghosts, and all he'd done about it was a big fat nothing.

Cook's body weight thudded against his leg. On reflex, Ant reached out to stroke his fur.

"Don't worry," he told the dog. "I'm not leaving her alone again."

THE WAY TO hell was paved with good intentions.

And Lily sure had had good intentions two days before.

"This is ridiculous," she said now, shooing away the reaching hands of someone else with good intentions. "I'm a little beat-up but I can get out of the car without your help. Thanks."

She knew her tone was flat—she *felt* flat—but Lily wasn't going to apologize.

She was grumpy, if she was being honest. Grumpy, hungry and in need of four walls around her that weren't lined with beeping machines.

Her helper rolled his eyes. He waved his hand, unperturbed.

"Just take my hand, Oscar the Grouch."

Lily gave Ant a look she hoped hurt, just a little. He'd been an orbiting planet to her sun for the past two days. She hadn't asked for the attention but she'd more than received it. When Ant wasn't at her home taking care of Cook, he was in her hospital room offering up theories on Arturo and the box, telling her stories of his life over the past fourteen years, or simply just sitting there, his face behind his phone.

It had driven Lily crazy.

She'd gone from a relatively solitary life to one where she hadn't been alone in days.

All thanks to one little explosion.

Lily let out a sigh. She stood tall after it.

The wrap on her ribs was tight; the dull pain of healing bruises made her stiff. She smiled at her house.

"Look how beautiful this *not*-hospital is. It should be on a postcard."

Ant laughed and let her go. A second later he was back with her bag in one hand and the other held out to her.

Lily wasn't having it.

"You've seen me walk on my own," she said. "I can manage it here."

"You also had to stay an extra day in the hospital because managing it alone wasn't something you should have been doing."

Lily grumbled beneath her breath.

"I'm sorry, I didn't catch that," Ant teased.

"I said, I only stayed to keep you and Juliet off my case. I don't need help now." She held her head high.

Ant didn't laugh again, or roll his eyes, but she thought he might be struggling to not smile. Regardless, she set out to keep her word. The walk to the garage door was a slow one, but one she managed with—dare she think it—grace.

That grace all but left when she laid eyes on Cook.

The dog was normally well-behaved but this was the longest they'd gone without seeing each other. Both parties got a little sloppy with their hellos. Cook almost toppled Lily over and Lily almost let him. It was only Ant who remained upright and strong. He put a hand between them to calm them both down and redirect them to the couch. Lily didn't realize until she was settled on a cushion that she was near tears.

Ant, thankfully, had excused himself upstairs with her bag.

Lily took the moment alone to reassure her best friend.

"I really am okay," she whispered to Cook. "Just a few bumps and bruises."

Cook lapped at her face. He'd barely settled by the time Ant had come back down.

"Bag is up, my car and your car are outside, Cook has been fed, walked and is mud-free, and *now* I'm hungry. You and your folks used to eat at Crisp's Kitchen a lot, right? Want me to order some lunch from there?"

Lily had been trying to keep her emotions off her face for as long as she could remember. It was habit. Necessary for her job, practical for her personal life. But during the past four days it had been more of an exercise than second nature. An exercise she found easier to fail in Ant's presence.

As he listed all the ways he was helping her, and still wanted to help her, Lily was caught between a myriad of emotions.

Ant was taking care of her.

She hadn't been taken care of in a long while.

Not since Ida was taken.

Lily's stomach betrayed her need to try to put distance between her confusion, gratefulness and long-planted guilt. It growled so loudly that Cook's ears perked up.

"I guess that would probably be a good idea," she relented.

Ant was pleased and stepped into the kitchen to place their order with a smile on his face and an almost-bounce to his step.

How long was he going to be with her?

How long was he going to stay in town?

Two questions that had stood tall in her mind over the past few days.

It didn't help that her professional questions weren't getting answered, either.

The workshop had indeed been a spot that Bryant Lautner had frequented, but the man himself was hard to find. Juliet and Kenneth had been searching through the internet, the town and local word-of-mouth. Last Lily had heard no one had been able to find out who owned the land Bryant's workshop was on. Or had been on. The lab within it had done a great job of destroying the rest of the house when everything went up in flames.

Everything, including the box of recorders.

Arturo had been questioned about them, about the workshop and his corresponding social media posts that had led Lily to investigate the property, but he'd clammed up quickly. Now he was in the county jail for assault and waiting for a trial. His bail had been set but not paid.

The man and the Cadillac outside the workshop?

Gone in the wind, though an all-points bulletin had been released to the public. She wasn't putting much stock in that panning out. The meth lab explosion had made the news quickly. If the man who'd started the fire had even one brain cell, he'd dumped the car right away.

It all ate at Lily.

She wasn't the only one.

Kenneth had visited her the day before and given his two cents on Arturo, the box in the ground, and the workshop's connection to Bryant.

"Kelby Creek might be small, but her confusing, complicated mysteries are mighty." He'd taken a moment to look down at his wedding band. "But we're patient and that counts for something."

Lily hadn't corrected him then.

Sometimes she was patient, but only because she'd had to be.

Right now, she didn't want to be patient.

Right now, she wanted answers.

Right now she—

"Hey, Lily?"

Ant's voice carried in from the kitchen. Less than a second later and Cook was up, alert.

She turned her head so quickly to the front of the house that the movement brought a searing pain. Lily clenched her teeth then spoke through them.

"Yeah?"

Ant came into view but only to walk to the front window. He looked almost comical as he spied through the curtains.

"Were you expecting any company?"

Cook joined him.

Lily could hear footsteps coming up the front porch stairs.

"No. I wasn't even expecting you to still be here," she said honestly.

Ant stood tall and gave her a look she couldn't decipher.

"Well then, you're definitely in for a surprise."

Chapter Twelve

"Coulrophobia."

Lily was in the kitchen, a newly poured cup of coffee in her hand. Ant was a breath away from her, head bent down so the new arrival in the living room couldn't hear them.

"Coulrophobia," he repeated back.

Lily nodded.

"That's what it's called—the phobia of clowns. A girl I knew in the academy had it. Broke down into a fit when someone brought in their bobblehead of Pennywise from Stephen King's *It*. She couldn't function until it was out of the building."

They both looked at the hallway separating them from the living room.

"Well it's a dang good thing we're not suffering from it, too."

Lily agreed.

"It would make questioning her less than ideal, that's for sure."

Lily handed Ant the coffee and grabbed her detective's notepad from the counter. Hurt or not, it didn't matter. Ant watched as Lily went from off the clock and wounded to ready-for-anything detective. That anything just so happened to be a young woman sitting on her couch in full clown makeup and costume.

"I'm so sorry again for the way I look," the young woman said as soon as they rounded the corner. "We have a show tonight at the fair and dress rehearsal is in an hour. I would have come over before costume and makeup but, uh, I wasn't even sure I was going to come until I was in the car."

Ant handed her the coffee.

The young woman took the cup and smiled shakily. Lily let her take a sip. She hadn't asked a question yet. Just invited the woman in when she'd told them she had to talk.

Lily instead looked at Ant, then motioned to the love seat.

At the nonverbal cue he pushed the love seat across the hardwood floor. It went from being next to the couch to across from it. Lily could now sit down opposite the woman, which she did. Ant took the seat next to Lily. He wasn't even sure the young woman registered either.

When she was done with her drink all she did was look at them for a moment before the rest of her words came out in a tumble.

It turned out Lily didn't have to ask any questions at all to get some answers. Maybe that's why she'd offered the coffee. She was simply waiting for the woman to find her ground.

"I'm—I'm Winnie. Uh, Winnie Johnson. I, um, I actually live in the neighborhood." She pointed over her shoulder. Her puffy, striped sleeves shifted. "On Kellogg Street, the house with the dark blue door in the middle of the block."

Lily nodded. "I've seen it. It's a nice door."

Her voice had changed. It had gone from annoyed at him, to flat when inviting Winnie in, and now it was soft. Not quiet, just soft. It seemed to encourage Winnie.

"Yeah, thanks." She laughed a little but there was nothing but nerves in it. She sobered after that. "That's how I knew where to come to see you, Miss Howard. Oh, sorry, Detective Howard."

"Lily's fine. And this is my friend Anthony."

Ant hadn't expected an introduction but he outstretched his hand and shook Winnie's with a smile.

The wobble in the woman's voice returned as she continued.

"I saw you, uh, when you moved in and Mrs. Claudine told me about you. That you were a detective. Me and my friend Kris—Kristine Cho—were curious and looked you up and found a few articles online about some cases you were on in Huntsville. The one where you were stabbed when you found that man trying to bury that jogger's body."

Ant tried to keep his cool at that.

He failed.

"You were stabbed?"

Lily didn't break composure. She nodded, all nonchalant.

"A man was stalking another woman when a jogger caught him by surprise. He was under the influence of some pretty intense narcotics and killed her. I responded to a call about screaming and found him trying to bury her in a shallow grave. Now he's in prison for life and I have a tiny scar. Both better outcomes than the woman's."

Ant knew his mouth was hanging open but he didn't comment again. Winnie kept on.

"Well, Kris just thought that was awesome. I mean, not the murder part, but how you manhandled this guy who was twice your size and drugged up. You see, we're in college. We go to the community college up the road and we've been trying to figure out what's next." Winnie laughed; it was self-deprecating. She waved her hand over her costume. "Clearly signing up to be a clown with the theater club wasn't what I imagined but well, it doesn't matter."

Winnie put her mug on the coffee table between them. Her hand shook.

"The reason why I'm here is because as far as I can tell, you're great at your job and you care and…well, you weren't here for The Flood. Which hopefully means you're not corrupt. I mean, I know there are others in the sheriff's department who are new and have come back to town to try and fix this place but a lot of us are still a bit weirded out by everything and—"

Lily reached out. Her hand rested on top of Winnie's forearm.

"Take a deep breath," she instructed. "In through the nose, out through the mouth."

Ant watched as both women did it together. Winnie's shoulders relaxed just enough to show that it had an effect.

She nodded when she was done.

"Now, tell me why you wanted to talk to me," Lily coaxed, her voice still as soft as a feather. A feather that weighed the same as a brick.

Winnie took another breath. Her entire demeanor changed.

"Kris left the fairgrounds early last night and now I can't find her." Winnie pulled her phone from her jumper's pocket. She unlocked it and held the screen up so they could see the picture. It was of Winnie and another young woman, their faces pressed together smiling while lights twinkled behind them. "It was the only night we could go without working so we went with a few people. But Kris left early. We drove there in my car because Monday night she got hers stuck in some mud out on Old Cherry Street and I kind of broke her bumper trying to tow her out. So when one of our friends saw her leave the fair early with someone, I didn't think much of it."

Ant had gone straight as an arrow. And it wasn't because the fair was the last thing he wanted to think about since once he thought about the fairgrounds, he thought about the woods behind it, and when he thought about the woods behind it, he thought about the creek. About the man. About Ida. He was sure Lily felt the same. Though she was much better at controlling her reaction.

She hadn't moved a muscle and when she spoke, her words sounded clear as day.

"You think she was taken from the fairgrounds against her will?"

Winnie shook her head.

"Our friend said she got into the passenger's seat without any issue but, well, one of the reasons I didn't go to the department with this is because Kris has had this secret boyfriend for a few months now." Winnie squirmed a little in her seat. "I mean she tells me everything but she gets all weird about talking about him so I… Well, I just kind of assumed he's married. So if I'm overreacting, and she just left with him and forgot her phone charger or something, and then I went to the department…"

"You're afraid you'd expose the affair," Lily finished.

Winnie nodded.

"I know that's not right but I wouldn't want to do that to Kris, especially since I don't even know that it *is* a married man." She put her phone back and gave one quick nod, seemingly to herself. Ant was surprised to hear her voice stronger than it had been since she arrived. "But I didn't want to *under*react either, not after what happened to you out at the meth lab."

Lily shared a quick look with Ant. The explosion had made the local paper and television news but he didn't get the connection between Winnie's friend and what had happened to them. Neither did Lily.

"What do you mean after what happened to us?" she asked. "Is Kris involved in drugs?"

Winnie was quick to shake her head.

"No, but my boyfriend told me this morning that whoever started the fire drove away in an old busted-up Cadillac." Winnie put her hands up quick in defense. "Uh, I'm dating Colton Dean. He's the EMT that drove y'all to the hospital. I swear he doesn't normally tell people stuff like that but, well, I kind of brought it up first."

Ant could tell Lily didn't like the breach of privacy. He could also tell she had already moved on when she spoke again.

"What about it?"

Winnie took on a pained expression.

Even through the white and red paint across her face, Ant could feel it.

Winnie didn't want her worry to be validated. She didn't want her fear to be real. She didn't want to believe something she already had started to believe.

Ant knew that feeling.

He knew that pain.

He felt it all over again when Winnie gave them their connection.

"The car that Kris left in last night was a Cadillac, busted up and old."

Winnie tried to smile. She wanted to be wrong. She wanted her gut feeling to be an overreaction. A girl crying wolf.

But Lily didn't jump in to reassure her that she had nothing to worry about.

That it was just a coincidence.

So Ant didn't see it as his place to lie, either.

LILY WAS OUT on her front porch directing an orchestra of law enforcement from the comfort of a dining room chair and her cell phone. Ant had brought it out when she'd insisted he stay inside and keep Winnie company.

"If she's comfortable with dogs, let Cook back in," Lily had told him, Kenneth's line already ringing in her ear. "He'll help her as long as you're friendly with her."

Ant hadn't questioned a thing.

Then Lily was bouncing between calls.

The first was with Kenneth and, after him initially reminding her that she was off duty for recovery, he paid rapt attention to what she had to say. A missing person was never a happy thing; a missing woman in Kelby Creek had become a lot more common than it should have been.

"She hasn't been missing an entire day yet," he pointed out, playing the devil's advocate. Lily knew it was necessary but she couldn't hold back the sharpness in her words when she replied.

"A twenty-year-old woman in a secret relationship gets into a car that matches the description of one driven by a person who set fire to a meth lab that has ties to both Arturo and Bryant. One of whom is in jail for assault on an officer after finding a buried box with a recording of a potential original tape of Annie McHale screaming during her ransom video. The other, a man I've been trying to find to question about the abduction of a sixteen year-old girl, fourteen years ago. I don't know about you but those sentences are so thick with suspicion I almost couldn't get them out."

"I'm not questioning how suspicious this all looks. I'm simply reminding you that, as you yourself just said, Arturo is in custody," Kenneth returned. "He's been there since Monday night. Kris entered the Cadillac yesterday, Wednesday night. We can work with theories but we need to also work with what we really have too."

Lily was hot under her metaphorical collar.

And she hadn't realized it until now.

Her emotions were twisting around her words, balling her hands into fists, clenching her teeth when she wasn't speaking.

She followed her own advice and took a quick but deep breath.

Throw the switch back to Off, she told herself. *Do what you're good at.*

"Well, with what we have I'd have Juliet keep looking for Bryant Lautner, you can keep looking into the recording and its connection to Annie McHale, and Foster can keep trying to find that car and go through the current narcotics scene in Kelby Creek for more information on the meth lab and suppliers who might know who was using it. I'd put Detective Reiner on Kristine Cho since he has a knack for finding people. Best case is she's with a married man and lost track of time."

"And what about you?" he asked.

Lily glanced at Winnie's car parked at the curb.

She pictured her blue door several streets away.

"I'm off duty, remember?"

Kenneth gave her the kindness of not prodding further and promised to keep her updated if and when they found something.

He also told her to stay safe.

Lily stood, careful of her injuries.

The ground had finally dried from Tuesday night's rain. Too bad for it that another storm was coming.

Too bad for whoever was in that Cadillac that Lily was coming, too.

Chapter Thirteen

It took some time but Ant and Lily finally convinced Winnie to go to the fairgrounds for her dress rehearsal.

They weren't certain that Kristine Cho was in danger, and even if she were, Winnie stressing over it wasn't going to help anyone.

So she'd gone and left them to do some investigating.

Ant blew out a low whistle when he and Lily stepped into Winnie and Kris's living room.

"How exactly do two twenty-year-old community college students get a place like this?" he asked. "If they sold it they could make a fortune."

Lily didn't laugh but she did point toward the fireplace's mantel.

"The secret for them is Winnie's parents. They're the owners."

Cole Reiner, a detective working with Foster, had given Lily a quick rundown on Winnie's parents before they'd left her house. It's how she knew they were into real estate and had gotten lucky with the stock market before leaving Kelby Creek a year ago. Kristine, on the other hand, had lost her parents in a car accident when she was seventeen. She had no other family. Just a best friend who was extremely worried.

Ant walked up to the fireplace and went over the pictures.

"Having parents who own more than one house isn't something you can market, I guess." He ducked his head around the corner to the stairs. "This place has almost the same layout as yours."

It was the exact same layout but decorated wholly differently. Where Lily lacked framed photos, fun little knickknacks and general color, Winnie and Kris had gone the extra mile. It gave the house a homey feeling, all warm and inviting.

That was why it looked different.

Winnie and Kris had a home that they truly lived in.

Lily stayed in a house.

"Winnie said Kris's room is on the right," she said. "Let's see if we can find something."

Lily took the lead but it was slow. She had a fresh painkiller in her but was still feeling stiff.

"I'm fine," she muttered over her shoulder, knowing that her every move was being monitored by the man behind her. "You can stop breathing on me."

Ant snorted.

"Maybe I'm just impatient," he said. "You're walking like this guy named Phil I met in Vegas when I was working at a club. He did this slow strut to let the ladies know he was single. Bless whoever's heart got stuck behind him."

Lily glazed over the Phil comment and went right for another surprise from Ant.

"You worked at a club in Vegas?"

"Yes, ma'am. One with a pool if you'd believe it. Everyone in swimsuits getting toasted."

Lily really wasn't liking the stairs. The discomfort didn't compare to her curiosity.

"You bartended at a pool club. In Vegas. Wearing a swimsuit."

"I was actually security. Bartending didn't happen until I was in Virginia."

Lily reached the landing. Ant was at her elbow. He didn't stay there long.

"Don't worry." He stepped around her to open the door and threw a grin her way. "I promise I still look great in a swimsuit."

Heat, true and fast, flourished in Lily's stomach. She didn't know how to handle it. Though she didn't have to struggle with the feeling long.

Kristine Cho's room wasn't an office. There wasn't a well-used whiteboard on one wall, several boxes with scrawled-on names on the floor, and there wasn't a desk in the middle where the young woman pored over old notes trying to find something that might not exist.

No, like with the floor beneath her room, Kris had taken the space and made it home. Although it wasn't all vibrant colors and warm sunshine.

The walls were a deep burgundy; the bedroom furniture was made of heavy oak and a little too big for the space. The throw across the bed had a kaleidoscope pattern but the colors were all deep shades. Framed pictures took up the top of the dresser beneath her window.

Lily went over to the pictures and traced each with her eyes before speaking.

"When Kristine's parents were killed she stayed with her uncle until she was eighteen, then moved in with Winnie soon after graduation." Lily motioned to the expensive bed frame. "If I had to guess, this furniture belonged to her parents."

Lily pointed back to the pictures on the dresser.

"And this is the spot I'm guessing that she reserves for pictures of only them." There were a few pictures taped to the wall over her nightstand, held up by colorful tape. Another few were over a small vanity set up along the wall next to the closet. "Anywhere else is fair game for pictures after they passed. Not this spot, though. I think this probably acts as a shrine of sorts."

Lily touched the top of the dresser lightly.

"Mom had a spot like that for Ida." Ant was bent down inspecting one of the pictures taped to the wall. "It was this little accent table thing in the living room and it was covered in pictures of her, like you'd see at a memorial service. She cleaned it twice a week and never put anything else on there. When she moved, it was the last thing she packed."

Lily's heart pulled a little. She tried to stay focused.

"I don't know who Kristine Cho was before her parents passed but I definitely think this is the room of someone trying to feel connected to her family. I'd bet all my paychecks that she even had this color wall in her childhood home." Lily wondered if Ant had kept his own ties to Ida. Did he have pictures of her on his walls at his apartment? Had he taken any of her childhood things with him as he moved around? Lily didn't ask. But she found she wanted to. The new urge to want to know more about him, to really know and not keep loose tabs on him, was surprising. "There's nothing wrong with trying to stay connected," she added on. "But it might help point us in the right direction of her secret romance."

Ant opened the vanity drawer.

"You think she might be dating someone who reminds her of her parents? That's a really weird offshoot of daddy issues, don't you think?"

"More like she could be craving stability, a sense of being taken care of," she answered. "One day she was just a teenager probably thinking about boys and school and her future. Then the next all she had was their furniture. I think that might make anyone want something in their life they can count on. Someone who makes them feel taken care of. Whether it's subconscious or not."

"So, probably not twenty-year-old boys," Ant concluded.

"Probably not."

Lily opened the young woman's closet.

Kristine's clothes were less somber than her room but not by much. She liked bodysuits, blouses that were in part sheer, and a few T-shirts that seemed to have sentimental value. There were a few summer dresses with floral patterns and next to those were fancier cuts and material. Lily ran her hand across a slinky black number with sequins. High heels sat beneath it in a clear plastic container.

Lily knew her pain meds were finally working when

bending down to get the box only felt stiff, not painful. She thought Ant was about to scold her for the move but turned to see him holding his own discovery.

It was a ring with a diamond so glaring that it stunned her to silence for a moment.

Though the fact that Ant was holding it out to her might have been the real reason she'd gone quiet.

And a little fluttery.

Only for the moment, though.

"I'm no expert on expensive, shiny things but if this isn't a fake I'm guessing it's more than two months of any paycheck I've ever gotten. Something I'd probably be showing off, not shoving into the back of a drawer."

Lily held up the plastic shoebox.

"These are Louboutin heels. They're also up there in price."

"Could the ring have belonged to her parents?" Ant asked. "And the shoes something she bought herself with their life insurance money?"

"It's possible. Let's keep looking."

She put the container on the bed and went back to the closet. Ant continued his search through the vanity. It wasn't long before he found a pair of diamond earrings in the second drawer and put them on the bed. Lily's search turned up two slinky lingerie numbers in the dresser. They looked new but she didn't pull them out for display. They were already invading her privacy. Even if Winnie had asked them to do it.

Lily went to the only place she hadn't yet searched on her side of the room. The nightstand had two drawers and matched the one on the other side of the bed.

Ant's search timed perfectly with Lily's. They shared a look as they stood in front of their respective pieces of furniture.

That fluttery feeling in Lily's stomach started up again.

She wasn't used to having a partner. Someone to be with instead of alone in her head. Someone who had no issues with being opposite her.

Someone who met her eye and held her after the world had exploded around her.

It was a strange feeling and one that surprised her again.

Lily tried to push it away but found it was as stubborn as the man who had put it there without knowing it.

But now wasn't the time to focus on her.

Both returned their gazes downward but Ant broke the silence they'd fallen into.

"Do you think what happened to us, what happened with Ida, really did affect us?"

The question was so broad and yet, at the same time, so direct that Lily didn't know how to answer. He must have sensed it.

"I mean with relationships, dating," he clarified. "I know I haven't been the best boyfriend in the past. I haven't really been a boyfriend all that much. The last woman I dated was a while ago and she told me I was 'commitment issues wrapped in denim.'" He chuckled. "Made me wonder about how many pairs of jeans I had then." A blink later his tone downshifted into somber. "Makes me wonder now if I've been a rolling stone all these years not because I couldn't find the right woman but because I never found Ida. Or maybe it's me I never quite found. I guess it can be hard to find yourself when you spend all of your years looking for someone else, huh?"

Lily's hands were hovering over one of the two open drawers in the nightstand.

Where had that come from?

How had they gone from searching a young woman's room to talking about this?

It was such a deep dissection made in such a casual way.

How was she supposed to respond?

How did she *want* to respond?

Had Ida's kidnapping taken a happy, mentally healthy young Lily and thrust her harshly into a world she neither trusted nor related to anymore—not unless she had a case in one hand and a tragedy in the other?

Had she simply gone through the motions of dating because it was expected?

Had Lily's decision to save Ant instead of Ida become a cloud above her head that always started to rain whenever she felt even a little bit happy, reminding her that Ida would never be able to do what she was doing?

Lily didn't know.

But, if she did, would she admit it to Ant of all people?

The silence became loud. It was only by training alone that the part of her brain that wasn't panicking was still looking for clues.

Lily's vision focused past her jumbling thoughts and finally onto the contents of the drawer.

There was something there that felt out of place.

"'Finnigan's at sunset.'"

"Come again?"

Lily held up the paper.

"It's a note," she answered. "Written on a torn-off corner of paper. It says 'Finnigan's at sunset.'"

The writing was in black ink. It was jagged. As if the writer had been in a rush or impatient. It could have been anything, it could have been nothing, but the hearts that had been drawn around the phrase were in pink highlighter and the kiss print in the corner was made from lipstick, a deep red.

"Is there anything you've seen in here that has Kristine's handwriting?" Lily asked. "Something we can compare this to?"

Ant was quick.

"Actually, yes. The Polaroids taped to the wall have names or captions written on the bottom."

They went to the other side of the room where Lily held up the note between two of the pictures. One caption read the month and year the picture was taken, the other read "Spring Break" with a heart and a sun drawing on either side.

"Not the same handwriting," Lily concluded.

Ant pointed to the drawings.

"But the hearts match up."

Lily placed the paper on the bed with the other items they'd collected.

"Extremely fancy shoes, an expensive ring, diamond earrings, new lingerie sets, and a note covered in someone else's handwriting but Kristine's heart doodles and probably lip print." Lily put her hands on her hips. "Without truly knowing Kristine I can't tell if she's dug in deep with the mantra of 'treat yourself' or these are gifts from a man neither one of them want anyone else to know about."

They shared another silence. Lily was getting frustrated. She stepped away from the items and focused on the note.

"'Finnigan's at sunset,'" she read again. "Is this a meeting place for the future or something that already happened?"

"It would have to have been in the last three days if it already happened."

Lily looked up at Ant, one eyebrow raised.

"You know what Finnigan's is?"

Ant's grin was sly.

"Only because Monica Glenn gave me my first kiss there." Lily wasn't amused. Ant explained. "It's the fair. Or part of it. Finnigan's Fun House."

"And the fair has only been open for three days," she realized.

"Yep. Well—" Ant checked the time on his phone "—technically two. I saw a flyer at the café. Tonight is armband night so they're not opening until five. We've got a few hours."

Lily went back to the note.

It, like the rest of the items in the room, just felt wrong.

The innocence of the doodled hearts and lip print didn't match with the expensive, more adult items.

And, maybe, that could have been Kristine's normal. She was a young woman who liked to doodle and then buy nice things.

But the fact was that Kristine Cho was also missing.

All together, none of it felt right.

"So, what's the plan, boss?" Ant's voice caught her off guard. He sounded excited. Enthused. Ready.

And there it was again.

That feeling of having someone with her. Someone close.

That feeling ran straight into the absolute fact that the man was also pure handsome. Being with him day in and day out had shown that not even the Off switch in her could deny that.

Lily shouldn't have felt heat at his words and attention, shouldn't have had to bite down on how it also made her feel more than what had been there before, but she did.

And she wanted to keep feeling it.

"Well, Ant Perez, it looks like we're going to the fair tonight."

HE THREW THE CHAIR.

He didn't kick it. He didn't push it. He didn't dramatically tip it.

He threw it across the room so hard that it shattered the display case against the opposite wall.

Trophies and awards broke, shifted and fell over at the disruption.

He didn't care.

"Human error," he roared at the bespectacled man

in the linen suit on the other side of his desk. "That's what this comes down to. Human error!"

He yelled again, a string of curses that made the other man flinch. Not that he wasn't already flinching without the less-than-polite words. He knew he'd messed up. He knew he'd collected consequences.

He knew that one more mistake would be the difference between his life and a less-than-ideal death.

Because, while he was great at his job on any other day of the week, his partner was the king of doling out consequences.

Consequences that came when the yelling finally stopped.

"Do you know how unobservant most people really are?" his partner asked, all volume and heat. "How gullible they are? How many actually look right and left before crossing the road?" He shook his head. "It takes so little to actually do a lot in this town and still you managed to get someone who messed that up."

Glass from the display cabinet crunched under the man's feet as he strode to the desk, seeming to stem his tirade. He sighed heavily and leaned over onto his desk, the tips of his fingers turning white at the pressure he was using against it.

"Idiots, pure idiots, have spent the last several years getting caught in the name of some kind of cartoon-worthy justice," he said, notably calmer. Though his quiet words managed to be worse than if he were yelling. "We are not idiots and I don't believe in justice. Fix your issues or I'll fix mine."

Though he wanted to shrink back, the man behind the desk maintained eye contact with his partner.

They both knew that the "mine" he was referring to was him.

"It'll get done," he assured him. "Then we can go underground for a while until this blows over. Just give me some time."

His partner was back to rage.

He struck his fist down hard.

"You had days. You had thousands of minutes, hundreds of opportunities, you had years, if we want to get technical. But what happened? *One* thing went wrong and then everything went wrong. Fix it. Or so help me, I'll burn you all."

He didn't say anything else and the man in the linen suit wasn't staying to chance it.

He left the room and didn't let out a shaky breath until he was outside.

He scurried through the parking lot toward his car, not caring that the dirt was no doubt staining his beige shoes.

His partner was wrong.

Their original problem hadn't been just one thing.

It had been two.

Detective Howard was back.

And she wasn't alone.

Chapter Fourteen

Cook was sitting at his side, the picture of patience. Ant finished washing the dishes in the sink with a laugh.

"I already snuck you some of my Crisp's chicken," he told the pooch. "I'm not about to let you lick the plate."

Cook didn't seem to appreciate that but stayed his course. He didn't even move when Lily appeared at the kitchen doorway with an exasperated sigh.

"Well, like I thought might be the case, no one at the sheriff's department was too happy with us poking around Winnie's house. They keep saying I need to rest and I keep saying they need to calm down because I have grade A painkillers and we don't have any idea what Kristine Cho is involved in because no one can seem to find her." Lily went from a sigh to a huff. She stayed in the doorway looking every bit as annoyed as she did focused.

She also looked like a woman in need of resting.

Painkillers or not, there was a tilt to her. A way she was cradling herself to offset her bruised and injured body. It was subtle but it was there.

But Ant wasn't going to join the chorus of people telling her to just sit it all out.

"But you told them what we found, right?" he asked, toweling off his hands. "You said that Cole guy was the one assigned to look for Kristine?"

Lily nodded. "I updated him first then called Kenneth, who looped in Foster."

"What about what they're doing? Anything on the land the workshop's on? The recorders?" Ant surprised himself. In all the commotion he'd forgotten to follow up with what she'd said in the ambulance. "And what about talking to the only McHale still in Kelby Creek?"

It had been the plan for Lily to talk to Darren McHale, Annie's uncle, about the recording and Arturo to see if there was any crossover, but then Lily had gone from a woman obsessed with finding the truth to a woman in need of medical help. Still, Ant couldn't believe he'd forgotten it. He'd just been so concerned about Lily.

That should have meant something to him but Ant didn't have the time to deep dive back into himself again. He'd already done that at Winnie's house, even talking about his past relationships, and *that* had been an unfiltered thought he wouldn't have normally shared otherwise.

Still, he would have been lying if he said he hadn't been hoping that Lily would open up about her past relationships. She might have been surprised at some of his former occupations, but he'd realized when she spoke about the man who had stabbed her in Huntsville that Ant knew even less about her life since he left Kelby Creek. And not just the trauma that might be lurking there.

He reined in those errant thoughts when Lily stepped farther into the room. "The job of questioning Darren McHale was scooped up by the sheriff. She spoke with him yesterday." Lily flashed a quick smile. "Apparently he's one of the main reasons the fair came back this year. He flashed some money incentives around and has been pretty involved. So involved that Sheriff Blake had to walk and talk with him when he was inspecting the place. She said somehow they wound up talking on the Ferris wheel."

Ant didn't know the new sheriff, not by reputation and not by name, but Lily must have liked her. There was no animosity in her words.

And there was the smile.

It was small but beautiful.

"As for all other leads, no one has been having luck," she continued. "Bryant Lautner was seen at Rosewater Inn a few weeks ago but after that he seems to have vanished. Arturo Hanson still won't talk and his lawyer isn't helping. Everything we were asking this morning is still unanswered. That isn't even counting our new questions."

Ant finished drying his hands with the towel and leaned against the counter. Cook seemed to have guessed that no more food was coming his way. He retreated to the other room.

"Kristine Cho, you mean," he said.

Lily nodded.

"I hope she doesn't fit into any of this but, if she

does, I'm not sure how." Frustration, clear and pointed, came through. It took the woman's frown and deepened it. "If the driver of the Cadillac is her mystery man and that mystery man is the one who set fire to the workshop, it's still not fitting for me. And our only connections between Arturo and Bryant are the recorders and the workshop."

"And don't forget Bryant has a small connection to what happened to Ida."

Lily met his eye.

"That small connection is a man coughing," she reminded him.

Ant was unmoved.

"And what's that phrase? 'The devil is in the details.'"

She didn't fight him on that. She didn't carry the line of conversation any further, either.

"We need answers," she concluded instead. "And I can't get them sitting here, waiting mindlessly." At the last word she reached up and touched a spot on her stomach. Her rib, more precisely.

He wondered if it was bothering her now.

He wondered if she would admit it if it was.

"Okay, well, maybe we don't wait around mindlessly." Ant pushed off the counter. "I may not have any degrees or a badge but I'm an expert at finding my way to a distraction."

Lily let out a noise of surprise as Ant took her hand and pulled her to the stairs. Cook appeared with an excited bark. Both followed him up. He didn't let go of Lily until they were in front of her bed.

It wasn't until they were standing there that Ant realized how promising distraction and then running a woman up to a bed probably looked.

One glance at Lily and it was clear that she'd reached the wrong impression. Her face was aflame. Red as a kiss.

She was a sight to behold.

A heat he hadn't felt in a long time ignited in Ant.

Maybe him running her to a bedroom wasn't all innocent intentions.

"I figured this would be easier on a flat but comfortable surface," he tried lamely to explain. Lily's eyes widened and Ant let out a nervous laugh. "What I mean to say is there's an exercise of sorts that works good for clearing the mind for a little while."

Lily's eyebrows went up so high it had to have hurt a little.

"I'm not doing myself any favors here, am I?" He motioned to the bed. It was impeccably made. He patted the spot on the left before walking around to the right. He made a show of taking off his shoes. "We're going to be witches for a bit."

Lily's deep crimson shade didn't get any deeper, and her sky-high eyebrows lowered. Her curiosity was easier to see now.

"Witches?"

Ant sat on the bed and then stretched out on his back. He stared up at the ceiling and put his hands on either side of his body, palms open to his sides.

"Do the same thing I'm doing and I'll walk you through it."

Ant wasn't looking at her but he just knew Lily was

hesitating. What he didn't know was if she would actually follow his lead.

Yet, after a moment, the bed sunk in a little next to him.

"Please tell me this isn't a pickup line," she said, adjusting herself. "Then please tell me if it is that it hasn't actually worked on anyone."

Ant laughed. It vibrated the bed.

"It's not a pickup line," he assured her. "It's not even a witch thing, I don't think." He paused. Smiling at the memory he was about to let her in on was easy. Feeling the weight of the reality that followed it was not.

"When Ida was thirteen she watched some teen movie about witches," he started, his eyes fixed on the ceiling above them. "I never watched it and couldn't even tell you what it was called. All I remember was that Ida and her little friends were obsessed, especially with some trick the teenagers in the movie did. 'It's called moving your power, Ant. Very serious stuff.'" Ant snorted. "She made me do it with her after everyone went home and, well, it just kind of became a thing we randomly did. I'd be in my room playing video games and she'd fling the door open and tell me it was time to be witches. Something, I have to point out, my mother wasn't a fan of. It wasn't until she did it once with us that she realized it was basically meditation. Meditation with a lot of talking."

He'd done this routine through the years whenever that ache in his chest became too much to bear. No matter where he was, he'd find a place to lie down and go through the motions while hearing Ida's voice walking him through it.

Such a silly little thing had become a tool for him to calm down.

He'd never told anyone about it, definitely never shown them how to do it before.

"Ready?" he asked.

Lily nodded. He felt it through the bed beneath them. "Ready."

Ant took a deep breath and let it out. Then he paraphrased his little sister.

"Power comes from the earth and your feet hit it first. So let's focus on our toes and make them tingle."

"Make them tingle?"

"With your mind, Lily," he said, all dramatic. "With your mind."

Ant felt the bed move a little as she laughed quietly.

"Oh, yeah. Sorry."

"It's okay," he said, adopting a deeper voice to really sell it. "I'll give you a moment to feel the tingle."

Ida had started to wiggle her toes at that point so Ant did that now. He tried to keep his smile in check when he noticed Lily doing the same.

"Now that we're tingling it's time to move that power from our toes to our heels and then spring it up to our knees," he continued. "Knees keep our legs together so it makes sense that they need to fill up. Let them fill up now, like bone bowls."

Lily let out a bite of laughter.

"Bone bowls?"

Ant *shh*ed her, trying to stay focused.

"Are those bowls filled? Good. Now it's time to pull that power to your belly. This is where the fun begins."

Lily followed his instruction. Ant continued on.

"Now we're going to close our eyes and make some decisions."

In the dark now, what had been fun and nostalgic was changing to a solemnness that weighted him down.

So he took the next part seriously.

"Take another deep breath and move that power to your heart. Really feel it. Really imagine that and nothing else. Then it's dealer's choice. You can move it to your arms next or go right on up to your head."

Ant felt Lily breathe in and out.

He tried to clear his thoughts, focus on his body—how he felt, how the bed felt beneath him, the AC vent blowing close enough that it brushed against his arm—but he couldn't.

"I never understood why the heart didn't get more time," he said after a moment. "We focused on knees but not the heart? Didn't seem that great of a plan." Ant's focus became full-fledged feeling. He missed his sister and had no way to fix that. Not even a witch's trick.

"One of the last times we did this together, I finally asked Ida why we didn't want the power there longer," he continued. "She told me that hearts are notorious for breaking. So why would you put all of your power there when you can put it somewhere more useful? I remember thinking how cynical that sounded from a sixteen-year-old who wasn't even dating anyone. Now, though, I guess I can see that logic."

Ant kept his eyes closed.

This was supposed to be a distraction, not a run and jump off the cliff into the past.

Ant was about to apologize and conclude their awkward meditation session but Lily spoke with notable vibrato.

"I went hands next because I use my brain all the time at work. I think they can definitely stand to get some more power in them. Where do you go next?"

Ant laughed, but even to his own ears the sound was strained.

"Head," he said. "I'm more of the opposite. I use my hands more than I ever use my brain."

Lily took Ant's right hand in hers.

"I'll let you borrow some of mine then."

She squeezed but didn't let go.

Ant didn't know how to react. Lily was a guarded woman. He hadn't expected her to reach out to him in any sense of the word. Not when he was the one who was trying to help clear her mind.

"So how do we finish?" Lily followed up. "What comes next?"

Almost all of Ant's focus was on their hands. The warmth and softness of hers.

For a moment he forgot the last step in Ida's exercise.

He cleared his throat.

"Fill the spots you haven't and then when that's done, don't say a word and inch it back through your body again. As Ida always said, 'A powerful body helps center a busy mind.'"

It sounded ridiculous.

Ant would have given anything to hear Ida try to convince him otherwise.

Lily kept his hand and Ant didn't let up his grip. Both grew quiet for a few minutes. He wasn't sure if the woman was actually imagining power going through her or if she was humoring him.

Either way, he gave her the privacy.

When Lily broke the silence, he gave her all of his attention.

"Did you know that after my twenty-third birthday I was dead set on joining the FBI?"

It was easy to be honest.

"No, I didn't know that," he answered. "That's impressive."

Lily shrugged.

"I just wanted to do more and everyone feels a certain way when they hear 'FBI' so I started the process of joining," she said. "I was excited and enjoyed it until I met another recruit named Grace. People at my last department used to say I was so quiet and brooding that I sunk the world around me, but Grace? She...was broken." Lily sighed. Ant held back his sudden anger at Lily's former colleagues.

"Grace's parents were attacked in an awful home invasion when she was twelve," she continued. "Grace was just small enough to hide in the dryer while her parents were tied up in the next room. The men killed her mother a few minutes later. Grace said she heard her scream but it was Grace's father's yelling for his wife that she'd never forget. It's what pulled her from her hiding space. She went to where she knew her father kept his gun, took it, snuck into the living room, crawled past her mom's body and then killed one of the men right then and there. The other man was so freaked out, he fled. Grace untied her father and the other man never came back."

Lily let out a low breath.

"The man who got away was the one who'd pulled the trigger on her mother and for years it drove Grace crazy. She looked for him everywhere, in everything. Nothing else mattered. Just finding him. It got so bad that Grace's father eventually moved them across the country until she went to college. Some little town in Maine where everyone knew everyone and no surprises ever happened.

"When I met Grace, she admitted that she'd probably never stop looking," Lily continued. "Even if she wanted to move on, she'd always be on the lookout for that man. One eye forever open. And I... Well, I felt that. But not as much as I felt it when she introduced me to her fiancé"

Ant chanced a look over at Lily. Her eyes were open but she was staring up. He could see her brow drawn, her lips downturned. She looked confused.

"Despite everything she had been through, despite her trauma and inability to let go, she managed to keep living. She managed to stay human."

Lily turned her head so she could meet his gaze.

"You asked me earlier if I thought what happened to Ida really affected us and our relationships," she said. "Before Grace I would have said yes. I would have said that I've been so focused on righting my wrong with Ida that I haven't had room for anything else. But then what about Grace? Have I been going through life using what happened as an excuse because it's easier?"

Ant wasn't sure she was looking for an answer so he didn't respond.

Lily didn't need him to.

She finished her story.

"That's when I realized that I wasn't ready to be Grace. And I, well, I didn't want to. All I wanted was to fix something. To undo my mistakes by helping others. And what better place to be when you want to fix mistakes and help others than Kelby Creek?"

"That's why you came back," Ant realized.

Lily nodded.

"If I can't find a way to live, I might as well be useful to those who can." She laughed a little; it wasn't all humor. "And I know that sounds dramatic but—"

Ant wasn't on any grade A painkillers for his bruised ribs. He could still feel the dull throb in them, in the bruises he had from the fight with Arturo and the explosion at the workshop. He also hadn't gotten a lot of sleep in the past few days and he'd be lying if he said he didn't feel that weighing him down a little.

Yet Ant felt nothing but ease as he moved across the bed and kissed Lily Howard right on the lips.

No pain.

None at all.

Chapter Fifteen

Life was strange.

One second you were moving power to your fingertips, the next you were kissing the one man in the entire world you never thought you'd kiss.

And enjoying it.

Lily's eyes fluttered as Ant ran his fingers along her jaw, pausing at her chin.

His lips felt like his hand in hers.

A little calloused but there was strength there and, like with the man himself, a surprising softness.

Ant wasn't just kissing her, he was caressing her with that kiss.

He was gentle.

He broke the kiss with the same carefulness.

Lily didn't want to open her eyes but she did.

Ant had propped himself up, which meant all Lily had to do to initiate another kiss was lean forward. An easy feat.

Instead, she couldn't help but fall to her insecurities.

"Why did you do that?" she asked, her voice breaking a little.

The kiss hadn't been long but it had been effective. Her entire body was still consumed by heat and nerves.

"Because you're not some ghost, Lily Howard." His hand found her check. His thumb rubbed a small circle, eliciting goose bumps across her arms. "You might be haunted but you're still alive. I know because you make me—"

Lily's phone blared to life in her jeans pocket. It took their intimate moment and shattered it with a gasp from her.

Ant dropped his hand and whatever he was about to say.

"I think you have a call to answer."

Lily sat up. She was hot. She was anxious. She wanted Ant to finish his sentence.

What she *did* was answer the phone.

"Hello?"

There was immediate silence. Lily pulled the phone away to make sure the call hadn't dropped. Then she heard a voice come through.

"Hi, is this Detective Lillian Howard?"

It was a man. He didn't sound familiar.

"Yes, this is she. May I ask who's calling?"

Ant sat up next to her. His eyebrow went high in question.

"I actually have information that I think you should know. It's about Arturo Hanson."

Lily shared a look with Ant. He motioned to his ears. He couldn't hear what the man had said. She held up her finger so he'd give her a minute.

"What kind of information?" She was careful not to sound too eager.

The man on the other end of the line was moving. There was a slight rustling sound coming through.

"I'd rather have this conversation in person. I feel like it would be safer to talk that way."

Lily struggled out of bed. Ant followed with more grace.

"Are you saying you're currently in danger?"

"No," the man said quickly. "I—I'd just rather do this face-to-face. It's hard to trust someone over the phone. Can we meet? In a half hour or so?"

Lily gave the phone an incredulous look. She kept her tone even.

"You haven't even told me your name."

The man hesitated.

"I…want to remain anonymous."

"I hate to break it to you, but the second I see you in person, that anonymity goes out the window," she pointed out.

The man didn't skip a beat.

"And when we're face-to-face you're going to realize why I want to remain anonymous for as long as I can." Impatience was clear in his tone. "Now, if you want to know about Arturo, meet me at Henderson Farm in a half hour."

Lily did a quick mental calculation.

"Next to the fairgrounds?"

"Yes, and Detective, come alone or it's no deal."

Red flags went from peeking out of the ground to up and at attention en masse.

"You won't tell me your name, you want me to meet you at an out-of-the-way location and you want me to come alone. I don't think that's—"

"And you want to know what Arturo wanted to do with that box," he interrupted. "Come alone or don't expect me to talk."

The phone call ended.

Lily pulled the cell away to look at the number.

It was blocked.

"What's going on?" Ant asked. "Who was that?"

Lily checked the time. It was two fifteen. Henderson Farm was twenty minutes out, not even technically a part of Dawn County, though it shared a plot of land with the fair.

"Lily."

Ant's voice grabbed her focus.

"Some man wants to meet me at Henderson Farm to give me information on Arturo. Just me. And he wants to stay anonymous until then."

Lily already knew Ant was going to be against the plan. What she didn't know was how much. He was off the bed in a flash, shaking his head.

"You're not thinking about doing that, are you?"

When Lily didn't instantly say no, his stance grew rigid.

"You know how in the movies when we know there's a trap set up for our heroes and we yell at the screen to not be that stupid? But then they're stupid anyway? This is one of those situations, Lily."

Lily matched his stance, getting out of bed, though a little bit slower.

"Are you calling me stupid?"

Ant blew out a frustrated breath.

"No. Lily, I—"

"Because the last time someone wanted to talk to just me, it worked out," she interrupted. "We wouldn't even know Kristine Cho was missing if not."

"Yeah but Winnie didn't give you a time, place and set of rules. She just showed up."

He had a point, but he was making it in a way that rubbed Lily wrong.

"You're acting like I've never been in a dangerous situation before," Lily said.

Ant put his hands on his hips in a move that showed nothing but exasperation.

"My God, you're really going to go out there alone, aren't you?"

"What if this guy just wants to remain anonymous and really does know something about Arturo?" she shot back. "I'll take my chances if that's the good outcome."

Ant's voice raised higher.

"And what about any other outcome? What if this guy is the guy we're looking for and he makes you disappear, too? You do remember the last two times you went somewhere alone, right? You were attacked and then *blown up*." He shook his head. *"No way, no way,* you're going alone. We go together."

Lily knew on some level that Ant was right. That going alone was foolish and everything about the situation sounded suspicious. Yet she couldn't stop the anger that inflamed her. For so many reasons and none of them Ant's fault.

But there he was.

Her only target.

"What *we*, Ant?" she yelled. "There is no *we*! I'm the detective, I'm the one whose job this is. Just because you follow me everywhere doesn't mean you belong here. This is my case and I can't keep entertaining you because I feel bad for you!"

All of Lily's guilt and anger and frustration melded together in another wave of true urgency. She hadn't meant to say exactly what she'd said but she was glad to see it had worked.

Ant's face went from angry to impassive in a flash. As if her words had wiped his expression clean.

Lily's chest rose and fell in fast breaths. Her heart rate was running a marathon.

Ant, however, looked calm.

He rolled his shoulders back and nodded.

"Fine," he said. "Then I'll leave."

He left the room without another word. Lily followed him but stopped at the top of the stairs.

Her heart hurt.

Her head told her to let him go.

She'd already caused him the pain of losing a sister. What was a little more?

Ant stopped at the first-floor landing. He turned around and met her stare.

His kiss already felt like a lifetime ago.

"Being desperate for answers isn't a good reason to

get killed, Lily. Promise me you'll at least tell someone at the department where you're going."

Lily thought of the dresser covered in pictures of Kristine Cho and her parents. The somber room and the too-big furniture.

She thought of the box. She thought of Arturo and his recorder. She thought of the workshop. She thought of the Cadillac.

They had no answers.

If there was even a chance that she could get one, wasn't the risk worth it?

"I'll call the sheriff," she said.

It was a lie.

But Ant took it with him as he left.

HALF AN HOUR LATER, on the dot, Lily was parking her car at the end of the drive for Henderson Farm. A minute after that she was standing next to her door and rubbing her finger along the scar on her side.

Winnie and Kristine's favorite story of Lily's takedown of Jeffrey Becker wasn't one she liked to talk about. Finding him trying to bury the body of a woman who had had an entire life ahead of her wasn't a good memory. Neither was the fight to get him into custody. Hence the scar that was rigid beneath her finger.

What most people didn't know was that Lily had to make a choice that night.

She'd been the first to arrive and was told to wait for backup. She hadn't. Instead Lily had hurried into the dark in hopes of saving whoever was in distress.

The victim was already gone but Lily had been able

to make her killer pay. Had she waited, that might not have been the case.

But then Arturo would have killed you with a shovel.

The voice in her head made Lily sigh into the cool afternoon air.

She'd gone alone to the woods and had only walked away because of Ant's interference.

There was no way to know what was the right choice until it was too late to change it.

Lily shook her shoulders back. She checked her service weapon at her hip, pulled her detective's badge out and made sure her phone was in her blazer pocket. She strode forward, hoping that Ant was wrong.

Henderson Farm used to be a dairy farm back in the early 2000s. Owned and operated by the Henderson family of six, its first building at the front of the land was their old home. Two stories, wraparound porch and faded red paint. Past the house were dirt roads that led to the barn and the old stalls. Lily had visited them on a field trip in middle school.

The Henderson patriarch had suffered an accident on the land that had put the family into financial ruin. That was until the McHale family had stepped in. They'd bought the land and whatever the price it had been enough for the Hendersons to leave Kelby Creek for a different life. Since the Hendersons had been well-liked, it had helped the town fall even more in love with the McHales.

Lily wondered if they would have finally made something of the farm if Annie had never been taken.

Now it looked beat-up and forgotten.

The perfect place to trap an unsuspecting victim.

Too bad Lily wasn't about that.

She pulled her service weapon out and held it low at her hip. Instead of going up to the front door, she walked around to the back, following the drive.

Nothing and no one made a sound.

There was, however, a vehicle parked by the back porch.

A white Cadillac in need of some upkeep. No tags.

Lily's adrenaline spiked.

She touched the back of the trunk. She couldn't see anyone through the back windshield. She walked around to the driver's side, not putting her back to the house. Last time she'd looked inside the Cadillac there hadn't been anything of note.

That wasn't the case now.

On the floorboard of the passenger seat Lily could see a few scattered pens. They were hollowed out. She spied a razor blade, too.

Both were common in meth use.

Lily heard Ant's anger in her head. His concern.

This wasn't just some source she was meeting.

This was the driver of the Cadillac.

The one who caused the explosion.

The one who'd almost killed her.

She put her gun in her holster long enough to pull out her phone. She cued up Kenneth's number.

It was only lucky that she hit Call just as the man walked out onto the back porch.

He had no holster but his gun was aimed squarely at her.

"Detective Howard?" he asked. "Did you come alone?"

Lily wasn't sure if Kenneth had picked up. She dropped her phone at the same time she replied so the man wouldn't hear it hit the dirt.

"Yes, I came alone." She spoke slowly and loudly. "Henderson Farm, by myself. I even got here in half an hour. I listened to your requests because I want to know what you know about Arturo Hanson. But why do you have a gun on me?"

Lily didn't recognize the man. Not even a little.

He was older, maybe late forties. A perfect tan, sculpted facial hair and a bald head that had a shine to it. He was dressed in business casual—a polo and khakis. Lily could see what looked like a Rolex on his wrist.

Whoever he was, he didn't fit with the Henderson house behind him.

Certainly not with the Cadillac.

He also didn't look comfortable with a gun, but that didn't stop him from using it as a threat.

"Walk toward me, slowly, or I'll shoot until I hit something."

Lily had already run her mental numbers. She might have had the car between her and the house but it wasn't a big car and it wasn't in the greatest of shape. She wasn't sure she could use it as cover.

And she really wanted to know who this guy was.

So Lily made another choice.

She just hoped it wasn't a bad one.

"Okay. Just don't shoot."

Lily left her phone in the dirt and walked slowly until she was in the Henderson house.

Chapter Sixteen

It was quaint, all things considered.

The back door led into the kitchen that passed through what seemed to act as an old office and then opened up to the entryway and the stairs. The furniture in each room looked maintained, albeit a bit dusty, and the walls, floors and tile were all in good shape. There was no peeling paint, no sagging ceilings, and definitely no meth labs. Just the most basic version of a house unlived in. But the lights worked. The air conditioner must have worked too because the coolness of the interior pushed into Lily's skin as she was told to walk up the stairs without making any sudden movements.

Whoever the man was, her opinion of him hadn't changed.

He was uncomfortable, not at all at ease.

There was sweat beading on his brow and no confidence in his game.

There also didn't feel like there was any experience in it.

The man hadn't asked for her phone and he hadn't

asked for the gun riding on her hip. Surely, he had to know it was there.

Lily wasn't going to bring it up, regardless.

She went up the stairs at a fast clip, the man scrambling to keep the pace. Lily ignored the pain that was pulsing in her ribs.

"The—the door straight ahead," the man said, his voice loud but not at all stable. "We can talk in there."

There were several doors before the one she was directed to go through, all of them closed.

Whether she believed the man might shoot her or not, not knowing what was in each room made her cool façade crack just a little. Last time she'd waited to open a closed door she'd ended up with singed clothes and broken ribs.

"This talk we're about to have, does it have to involve the gun?" Lily was at the door at the end of the hall. She stopped.

"I need it so you'll listen. Now go."

Relief poured through Lily at seeing a room that was neither a meth lab nor some type of torture scene. Instead it was an attic space that had been renovated into a bedroom. It was long but narrow, with the ceiling lowering on either side, and had two twin bed frames pushed up against the opposite walls. There was one window. It looked over the property behind the house, showing the high grass of a farm that hadn't been as well-kept as the main house.

The man surprised Lily by walking around her and stopping in front of the window. The gray skies emitted a natural light that framed him and his gun and cast the room in an almost eerie glow.

It also made Lily's opinion of the man change slightly. He didn't just lack the confidence and practice to do what he was doing—he also looked very much like a man who didn't want to be there.

But he was there and so was Lily. It was time they dropped their pretenses.

"I want to know who you are, if that's your Cadillac out back and what it is that you know about Arturo Hanson," she commanded.

Lily expected the man to offer a clever little spiel, the downfall of many egotistical men up to no good, yet he surprised her.

"My name is Jacob Anderson. I know Arturo because he's been trying to stop me from distributing meth in his territory. I didn't listen. So he threatened my mistress, Kristine Cho, and even though he was caught, his partner carried the threat through. Now she's gone."

Lily threw her mental switch that kept her emotions from reacting. She took on a clinical, calm tone.

"What do you mean, she's gone? Where is Kristine?"

Jacob shook his head. His gun bobbed up and down.

"It was a mistake," he said. His eyes were not even on her but somewhere on the ceiling, as if he was recalling something. "An accident. I wasn't even supposed to be there. I—" He stopped himself and his gaze snapped back to Lily. "Arturo put the box in the ground as a bluff to show me what would happen if I didn't stop my operation, but I didn't get there before you showed up. I was enraged when I found out and wanted to send my own message by burning down his lab. I didn't know he had a partner." He let out a breath that shook. "If I had... I wouldn't have said anything. Done anything. I wouldn't have stayed."

Lily took a chance. She slid her foot forward to get her an inch closer. The small movement focused Jacob's attention.

"Who is Arturo's partner?" she asked, softening her voice to nearly a whisper. "And, Jacob, where is Kristine?"

Lily's gut started to overturn her original thought that he wouldn't use his gun. The man's eyes became wide and wild. He was degrading at an alarming pace.

"Arturo was working with Bryant Lautner." His voice broke. His eyes were starting to tear up. Lily's read on the man fell with the drop of her stomach.

If he was this upset... What had happened to Kristine?

"I didn't know he had a partner," he repeated before Lily could say a word. "I didn't know."

Jacob brought his gun up to his head.

Lily didn't hesitate.

She pulled hers out and aimed it at the man.

"Stop," she yelled. "Please."

Jacob kept her stare, the barrel of his gun against his temple.

"Kristine is gone."

"She's not just gone, Jacob. She is somewhere no matter what happened. *Please* put the gun down and tell me."

He shook his head.

Lily dug in, hoping to play on the man's feelings for his young lover. "Think about her, think about Kristine. Think about everything she's been through. Think about how she deserves more than this. Think about Finnigan's at sunset."

Jacob's brow pulled in, like he'd heard a sound he couldn't place.

Like he was confused.

Like part of him wanted the pain to end and the other wanted to do right by the woman he loved.

A quiet settled between them.

Then, slowly, Jacob started to lower the gun.

"Thank you," Lily told him, meaning it.

Jacob shook his head again.

All at once every part of him that had felt off and broken became firm and confident. His words next had no break in them. Had no waver.

He was just a man giving her a message.

"Tell her I love her."

Lily yelled out but it was too late.

The gunshot was so loud it felt like the entire world had to have heard it.

Somehow, though, the silence that followed still managed to be louder.

THE "WELCOME TO KELBY CREEK" sign was in his rearview and the Holiday Inn's "Vacancy" was blinking in front of him when Ant thought about mud and put his Camaro in reverse.

He was still thinking about mud when Winnie answered her door ten minutes later.

She'd taken off her clown costume but some of her makeup still lingered. If Ant hadn't already seen her earlier that day, it would have given him pause. Now he was just glad she was home.

"Monday there was a big storm and you said you had to tow Kristine's car out of the mud, right?"

Winnie didn't ask any questions, just answered.

"Yeah. She wasn't too deep in so I thought I could do it," she said. "I mean, I did get her out. I just kind of broke her bumper. The car is still at Davie's Automotive."

"And she was stuck on Old Cherry Street?" Winnie nodded. "Did she tell you why she was on Old Cherry Street?"

Winnie's brows drew together in thought.

"She said she was using it as a shortcut to the fairgrounds. She left part of her costume in the theater trailer and wanted to clean it. After it took us forever to get her car out, she waited until Tuesday morning instead."

Ant could have been on to nothing or he could have finally found something useful.

"Unless there's another Old Cherry Street that I don't know about or the fairgrounds have moved, that's not a shortcut to the fair," he said. "There's really no shortcut. You just make it to the main road and boom, you're there."

Winnie's eyes widened.

"Oh my God, you're right. I—I didn't even question it."

Ant nodded. "Okay, well, thanks. I just wanted to ask."

He started to turn but Winnie caught his arm.

"Where are you going? Are you going out there?"

She let him go but he understood the look she was giving him. There was a lead. Small but there.

It was blood in the water and they were sharks hungry for the truth.

"Yeah," he said. "I'm going to see if there's anything interesting on Old Cherry Street. It's been a long time since I've actually driven it."

Winnie ducked back into the house and disappeared from view for a moment. When she reappeared she had on a rain jacket and held her keys.

"Can I come with you?"

"There's probably nothing out there," Ant tried. "It would just bother me if I didn't at least look."

"Well, I can tell you that there's nothing in here worth me doing," she replied. "I didn't even stay at dress rehearsal. After that detective that Lily sent started asking everyone questions it all became too real. I've just been sitting in the kitchen, staring at the wall ever since. I'd rather try to do something productive."

Ant sighed. Then he nodded.

"Let's go then before it decides to rain again."

Winnie locked up the house and bounded to the car. It wasn't until they were driving out of Holly Grove that she thought to ask about Lily.

"Did she find something, too? Is that why she isn't here?"

Ant bit down on a grumble.

"She's working a lead, yeah," he sidestepped. "It's

more official than looking at a once-muddy road so we split up."

Winnie didn't question that. She did, however, give him a look that made Ant uncomfortable. It was as if she was seeing him differently than the last time they'd talked. Before he could ask her about it, she spoke.

"I, uh, I looked you up earlier," she said. "I mean I knew about Lily's career record and even found the story about her fighting a kidnapper here in Kelby Creek when she was seventeen, but I didn't realize— I didn't put it together when I first met you that it was your sister. The girl who was kidnapped. And, well, that you two tried to stop her abductor. I—I can't even imagine."

Ant gave a stiff nod.

"It's not something we like to talk about."

"I don't blame you, but I— Well, I just thought that it was kind of nice that the two of you—you and Lily— are still fighting crime together. Or, I guess, still trying to help others together." He saw her shrug out of his periphery. "Y'all stuck together. Y'all must be close."

Ant kept driving, going through the last light they'd pass before the roads started branching off and asphalt turned to dirt.

He didn't know what to say.

He didn't want to lie.

He didn't know what the truth was.

"Lily is the only woman who's ever made me nervous and I can't say I know why." Ant surprised himself with that. "I've spent the last fourteen years knowing other women, trying at relationships, and feeling, and not feeling, all sorts of things. But one look at Lily? I get all jumpy inside. It's not just jumpy, either. She frustrates me like no one else but I'm proud to know her, more than I'm proud of even myself. She's spent over a decade trying to solve everyone's issues and I bet she thinks working on herself is a luxury. Something she can't do until all the cars have left the lot and the lights have been switched off," Ant grumbled. "The fact is that being with her should feel like losing Ida all over again but it doesn't."

Their fight had affected him more than any one thing had since he'd left Kelby Creek as a young adult. A little while ago he'd packed up and left, stung at her words. At the feeling behind them.

At the fact that she had been right.

He had shown up and then hadn't left.

She had never asked him to stay.

Ant gripped the steering wheel.

Then he let that grip loosen.

He sighed.

"You had it right. Being with Lily feels nice…and I don't think I've ever actually told her that."

There it was.

How he was feeling boiled down into a conversation with a woman he barely knew on the way to look at mud.

He gave Winnie a quick look.

"Sorry," he told her. "I guess I need to get better at communicating."

Winnie was smiling.

"No problem," she said. "If it makes you feel better,

when Colton first told me he loved me it was during a fight about him eating my leftovers out of the fridge. Sometimes you just don't know how you feel until you accidentally say it."

Ant was about to point out he hadn't said anything about love but the road sign for Old Cherry Street came into view.

Winnie's smile dropped. They were nothing but focused driving down the old road. Winnie was quiet until she pointed out the tire marks that were still there.

"That's from me," she said. "I pulled up next to her because I was afraid to get on the shoulder behind her. I don't have the best nighttime vision and didn't want to chance us both getting stuck."

Ant pulled over and threw on his flashers. They got out into the falling chill of the day.

"She was stopped on the side of the road?" Ant walked over to the tracks. Old Cherry Street was a dirt road in the trees for half of its expanse. The other half had grass fields if he was remembering correctly. There weren't even streetlights along the four-mile drive.

"Yeah," Winnie answered but that answer turned into an uncertain statement. "But why was she stopped here at all? Why did she pull to the side of the road?"

Ant's thoughts exactly.

There was no real reason to take Old Cherry Street as a shortcut to the fairgrounds. There was even less reason to stop on it.

Winnie let out a small yell of frustration.

She had her hands in her hair.

"How could I not ask about any of this?" she cried

out. "Why didn't I question it? I just came out here, *laughed* at the fact that she got stuck, and then joked about it when we got home. How oblivious can one person be?"

"This could still be nothing," he reminded her. "And even if it isn't, this isn't your fault."

Winnie didn't look so sure.

She turned to stare down the road ahead.

"I've lived in Kelby Creek all my life and I don't even know what's at the other end of this dumb street! But how could I not realize that it definitely wasn't the fair?"

Ant went over to the young woman. He tried to be soothing.

"The only thing in that direction of town are two neighborhoods that you wouldn't visit unless you're flush with cash."

Winnie gave him a questioning look.

"The country club, the Justine Park subdivision, and the McHale mansion are that way. Old Cherry connects to the nicely paved street that never has potholes that loops in front of all three." Ant stopped himself. Winnie picked up the thought.

"Somewhere a married man with money who was having an affair might live."

Ant looked at Old Cherry differently now.

"She could have been meeting him here," he said. "Halfway between your place and his."

They both chewed on that for a minute. Before Ant could decide what to do next, his phone rang in his pocket.

He pulled it out. The ID read Unknown.

He'd hoped it was Lily.

"Hello?"

"Hey, Anthony? This is Kathryn Juliet. Are you still in town?"

Ant might have trouble with sharing his feelings but right then and there he knew he felt nothing but pure worry.

"I am. What's wrong?"

The detective's voice lowered to a whisper. It set him even further on edge.

"We need to talk."

Chapter Seventeen

Cook was leaning heavy against her. He'd already nudged her hand several times. He was a weight, a pressure, an attempted comfort. Now he was trying his best to take the pain from his human and change it into something else. Something happier.

Something less *numb*.

Lily stared at the tabletop and the holster resting there. Her detective's badge was next to it.

Her phone was by her hand. No one had called her. They didn't need to since she'd left the department.

Jacob Anderson was dead. Bryant Lautner was still in the wind. The Henderson Farm had law all over it. The search for Kristine Cho did, too.

All Lily had was an awful feeling in her gut, literal blood on her arm and three words on repeat in her head.

Kristine is gone.

Lily balled her hand on the table.

Cook whined.

She didn't know Kristine, hadn't even heard the name until that morning, but all of her ached for the woman. After losing her parents she had deserved a lifetime of better and what had she gotten instead? Used as a pawn between two drug dealers.

Lily hated it.

She hated all of it.

Cook shifted against her leg. Lily thought it was his training trying to sway her to a lighter place but he was looking toward the front of the house.

That's when she heard the car door shut.

Lily sighed and dragged herself up and out of the chair. Despite telling him to leave, she knew it would be Ant stopping by. Juliet had at least given her a heads-up that she'd called him.

"You need a friend," she'd told her. "He seems to be a good one."

Lily hadn't corrected the woman then—hadn't told her that all Ant was, was a man who had gone through a trauma with her and then gotten pulled into another—but she fully intended to let Ant off the hook now.

If he wanted to stay in town until Bryant Lautner was found for Kristine's sake and then the questioning of his connection to Ida's abduction?

That was fine.

If he wanted to stay in town because he thought she needed protecting? That she needed his help? His concern?

No.

She'd kindly turn him around and remind him that she'd made it fourteen years without needing someone. She could make it through this.

Lily gave Cook a pat and was at the door just as a knock sounded.

She opened it wide and, sure enough, there he was.

Anthony Perez.

Dark hair.

Dark eyes.

Once a boy in her lap, the creek behind them.

Lily opened her mouth to tell him to go. To tell him she was fine. To tell him something.

Yet the words never came.

One look at Ant and Lily did something she hadn't done before.

She let go.

A sob was the first thing to tear itself out of her. The tears came next. In between the two there was Ant.

He pulled her into his chest without a word. When Lily went limp against him, he scooped her up gently, lifting her off the ground and stepping inside the house.

She didn't hear the door shut behind them. She didn't notice the stairs passing beneath them. She didn't even register the water turning on in the shower until the water was hitting her.

Hitting both of them.

Lily watched between her sobs as blood and mud swirled down the drain.

She felt the washcloth on her arm and then on her face.

Jacob Anderson's blood.

Lily lost it after that. Truly and completely.

That numb feeling had exploded into anger, regret, pain.

From witnessing what she had, to Kristine Cho's fate, to the pain of her injuries, and all the way to hearing Ida scream for the first time.

It all was too much.

And Ant somehow knew that.

He took over completely, drying her off, helping her change and then placing her right into bed.

"You're going to be okay," he told her, pulling the covers up over her.

He stepped back. Lily wasn't sure if he was just giving her space or if he meant to leave, but she didn't like either option.

She grabbed his hand.

Not only had Lily finally let go, she had another surprising first.

She asked someone to stay.

"Don't leave."

Her words were broken and cracked, filled with tears and, at the same time, drained of them. She knew she didn't look much better. She understood it wasn't just the outside of her that was showing how vulnerable she was.

If he left? If Ant walked out of the room?

It would be okay.

It would—

Ant walked around to the other side of the bed and slipped beneath the covers. His arm, unbelievably warm, wrapped around her shivering body. He pulled her against his chest.

Lily felt his heartbeat pulse through her.

Then she cried herself to sleep.

SOMEONE'S PHONE WAS VIBRATING.

Ant pictured his cell phone on his nightstand and

tried to flip over and slap at it. Something kept him from doing it. A few seconds passed before he realized that something was a woman.

Lily.

They were in her bed.

That was her phone vibrating on her nightstand.

She stirred, still pinned to him by his arm around her waist. Ant lifted it up just as her movements became more coordinated. She threw her legs over the bed and made a noise that let him know she'd hurt herself. Ant didn't say anything, though. Lily cleared her throat, answered the phone and then crept to the bathroom to talk.

She hadn't realized Ant was awake.

He hadn't realized when Juliet had called him the second time to tell him that Lily was home that he'd be in her bed later.

Ant rolled onto his back. The room was dark. No sunlight or afternoon glow filtered in between the curtains. Based on how he felt, he guessed they'd been asleep for a few hours at least. He hadn't known how much he needed it until Lily's breathing had evened out against him. After that? Her momentary peace had been a lullaby that had taken him under quick.

And kept him under apparently.

He stretched and wondered if he should get up.

He toyed with the decision until he heard water running in the bathroom sink. Shortly after, Lily was back in the bedroom. She put her phone back on the nightstand and slid carefully back beneath the sheets.

She was quiet a moment.

Then she whispered into the darkness.

"Are you awake?"

He nodded then realized she couldn't see him.

"I am."

"Oh. Sorry," she said. "That was Kenneth."

Ant sat up a little.

"Is everything okay?"

The bed moved as Lily shifted her weight. A second later the lamp on her nightstand came on. It wasn't bright but it still made Ant blink a few times. It also showed him Lily's very swollen eyes.

He wanted to reach out but, considering they'd just woken tangled up together, he didn't want to keep crowding her.

"He wanted to update me on what they'd found since I left. Wait, how much did Juliet tell you about what happened?"

There was no reason to lie.

"Everything you told her when she and Kenneth showed up at the farm."

"Everything?"

He nodded.

"She said if you trust me, she trusts me. Plus, she figured you'd tell me anyway."

Juliet had also said she wanted him to be prepared when he saw Lily again. She'd been too quiet at the farm, too quiet at the department. It had worried Juliet. Ant refrained from telling her all of that, though.

Lily let out a small sigh.

"Then you know Jacob Anderson admitted to being Kristine's boyfriend." He nodded. "And that he admitted to fighting with Arturo." He nodded again.

"Yeah, and that Bryant Lautner was Arturo's partner and that, best as anyone can guess, he's the one who took Kristine from Jacob at some point after they left the fair together last night."

Lily looked surprised.

"She really did tell you everything." She shook her head to get back on track. "They're still looking for Kris and Bryant but Foster went to Jacob Anderson's house and they found evidence to support the affair, including receipts for all of the things in her room that were expensive like the earrings, shoes, and lingerie. I think he said something about pictures of Kris on Jacob's computer too. His wife had no idea about the relationship or the drug dealing. They were high school sweethearts and she said he didn't even smoke cigarettes."

"It's never the people you suspect, I guess," Ant said.

Lily agreed with that.

"Apparently news of what happened made it to Arturo," she continued. "He requested a meeting with Sheriff Blake and a few minutes ago confirmed everything Jacob told me. He's been feuding with Jacob over territory and after he caught him and Kris together, he decided to try and use her against him. He never counted on a hunter finding the hole or us finding the box. He also never counted on being taken into custody. After that he guessed Bryant escalated."

Lily's face fell.

"It's not your fault that Bryant went after Kris," Ant jumped in. "I know that's what you're thinking but Arturo is the one who attacked us. You did your job. None of what happened next was your fault."

Ant wasn't sure if his reasoning landed. He wasn't the only one who had tried it.

"Kenneth said the same thing," she admitted. "He also told me, in not so many words, to not leave this house unless it was an emergency *but* that he'd let me know if anything happened."

Lily let out another sigh. This time she sank back into her pillow.

"Normally, I would have laughed at the order to stay home. But, I guess, having a breakdown puts things into perspective."

Ant rolled onto his back and joined her in staring at the ceiling, just as they had done earlier.

It was amazing how much had changed since then.

"Speaking of which, thank you," Lily added. "I didn't expect to lose it like that."

Ant shrugged.

"I don't think anyone ever does."

They shared a companionable silence.

But then things started to change.

Ant was in his briefs. Only his briefs. He'd taken off his wet clothes after the shower but hadn't had the chance to get dry ones from his backpack. Not when a wet and shivering Lily had needed him. He'd made fast work of dressing her in the first nightshirt and panties he'd found in her dresser.

Had he seen her naked?

Yes.

Had it been anything other than technical work?

No.

Now? Now Lily wasn't crying. She wasn't shivering. She didn't have blood on her from a dead man.

She was next to him, breathing easier, and he could still feel her warmth against him.

Ant went from feelings of being protective to feelings that ran more carnal.

It wasn't the time.

Yet he turned his head to face her all the same.

Lily was already looking at him.

Even in the dim light her eyes still managed to pull all of him in.

His gaze traveled to her lips as she spoke.

"When we were being witches, you told me that I wasn't some ghost. That I was alive because I made you…something. You never finished." She tilted her head a little against the pillow. "What were you going to say?"

Ant didn't pretend that he couldn't remember.

"I know you're alive because you make *me* feel alive when I'm with you."

It was the truth.

Just as he'd told Winnie in his accidental confession.

The past week had felt wholly different than the past fourteen years.

The only difference?

Lillian Howard.

She shook her head. Her hair shifted and trailed down the pillow at the movement.

"You only feel alive with me because you feel some misplaced obligation to me." Her voice was soft but strained. "Because I saved you from the creek. But, Anthony, I *need* you to remember what happened. I *need* you to remember that I'm the reason Ida was taken. I'm the reason she's gone."

It wasn't like earlier. The tears that came were few. They slid, one by one, down Lily's cheeks.

It wasn't a chaotic burst of emotion. It wasn't a bottle finally uncorked.

It was long-standing pain.

It was something that Lily had been living with since that night in the woods.

And, once again, Ant hadn't seen it until now.

"Oh, Lily." He reached out and cradled her face in his hand. "You didn't choose me over Ida. There was no choice at all. You saved the only person you could."

He pushed up on his elbow so he was looking down at her. Ant wanted to make sure she saw his sincerity. He smiled. "I have *never* blamed you for not going after Ida and I'm so sorry I didn't tell you that then. It just never crossed my mind that you would blame yourself because I, well, I don't. Not once. Not ever."

Ant ran a strand of her hair behind her ear.

"We shouldn't have had to live that night and I know it's changed us from whatever we might've been, but I can't help but be grateful for where it's led us. Where it's led me." Ant tipped Lily's chin up with his fingers. She let him kiss her softly. Then he was back to staring down at her. "But I'm not the only one who lived through it. I didn't have to save a boy. I didn't have to see a girl being pulled away into the darkness and think that I was the reason behind it. So, if being with me is too hard, tell me. I'll leave. Just know that, no matter what, I was truly happy here. With you. And not because of some misplaced obligation."

Ant released his hold on her. He meant every word he'd said.

It was selfish to want to be with Lily. He saw that now. Just because he felt alive around her didn't mean she was feeling the same.

He'd leave.

Lily didn't say anything for a moment.

When she did speak, it was on the tail of a deep exhale.

And it was just one word.

"Stay."

Chapter Eighteen

It was Lily's turn to show Ant just how much she'd been fighting against him until now.

The moment he smiled at her admission that she wanted him to stay, it was all over for her.

Lily wrapped her arm around his back and laced her fingers into his hair. She pulled his head down and let his kiss devour her.

There was no pulling away now.

No ill-timed phone calls or heartbreaking worries.

Ant didn't blame her for saving him and not running after Ida.

He had never blamed her.

And Lily believed him.

Ant dropped his hand to her waist. It trailed up her side beneath her shirt. Lily moved up against him. His chest was hard, unmovable.

Just what she wanted.

As their kiss turned deep, Lily pulled him on top of her. A second later she remembered her ribs might not like that. Thankfully, Ant had already thought ahead.

He made a cage around her, keeping his weight off her upper body.

His lower half, however, was right where it needed to be. Lily wrapped her legs around him to straddle the hardness of his pleasure.

She moaned against his lips.

When Ant pulled back, she almost groaned in anger.

"I don't want to hurt you," he breathed out, ragged. "Tell me if you want me to stop."

But Lily merely pulled him back down to her.

That was the golden ticket for the rest of the ride. Ant didn't stop them again, he didn't ask if she was okay, and when Lily yelled out later he didn't hesitate, thinking he'd hurt her.

Instead the two of them found a rhythm, a pulse, an understanding.

A connection that didn't include a creek or rain or darkness.

It was something completely new, something only for the two of them.

And, when their breathing calmed and their bodies relaxed, Lily knew she didn't want whatever they had just become to end.

It had been a long, long time since she'd gone to bed with a smile on her face.

But she did that night, even as worries of the future tried to claw their way in.

IT WAS FRIDAY at noon and the sun felt like only a memory. Lily was in the backyard before the inevitable rain, with Cook and Sheriff Bennet.

Neither woman was wearing her usual uniform but they were together to talk about work. That much was made clear when the sheriff called to ask for a moment. Now was that moment and Lily looked across her patio set with an anxiousness she felt to her bones.

"You know, when I first was elected to this job, to this town, I knew it would be a ride," the sheriff started after they'd exhausted all the niceties in Southern greetings. "I was even told after the fact to watch out because you could be clear sailin' on a Monday and then have the world flip three different ways by Friday. That's just how this town has become since The Flood. I guess I thought everyone was being overdramatic." She sighed, drank some of the coffee that Lily had prepared for them and slid right into what she really wanted to talk about.

"We found Bryant Lautner this morning." Lily sat straighter. Her ribs complained at the move. The sheriff raised her hand in a "stop" motion. "It was my call not to loop you in until now but I wanted to come over and tell you what we learned face-to-face because you earned that much."

Lily tried to keep her emotions in check.

"Okay."

Sheriff Bennet nodded then got to it.

"He didn't say much in the beginning. He denied taking Kristine and he stuck to silence when we asked where he had been prior to us picking him up." The sheriff readjusted her matter-of-fact tone to what Lily might describe as a warmer approach. "The first answer we got was to his whereabouts fourteen years ago, the day that Ida Perez went missing."

Lily felt her eyes widen in surprise.

The sheriff continued.

"Gray told me about the lead you were chasing with Bryant before all of this mess came to light, said that was why Anthony was here too most likely. He said you should have been the one asking but if you weren't there, he wasn't leaving until he at least did." She snorted. "Detective Lovett also pointed out how it could be relevant, and who am I to fight that?"

Lily was touched. Kenneth had fought for her. Foster, too.

That meant something to her. She'd have to tell them later.

"What did Bryant say?"

The sheriff's warmth became something more clinical. Lily knew it wasn't the news she wanted to hear even before she said it.

"He knew exactly where he was because he was on the way to his mother's funeral. The funeral home hasn't changed in over three decades so it wasn't too hard to confirm. I did it myself, actually. Pulled the old director out of bed and we looked into his files. Bryant was seen by several witnesses at the funeral that afternoon, the memorial at his mother's house after and the bar that night. Deputy Costner even took it a step further and found an old girlfriend of Bryant's who said he spent the next day passed out and then hung over."

Lily sighed.

"Which means Bryant Lautner didn't abduct Ida."

The sheriff shook her head.

"Not unless he could be in two places at once, no."

Lily sat with that for a minute. She didn't know what to feel so she did what she always did. Focused on the case at hand.

"Bryant didn't say anything else?" Lily asked. "About Kristine?"

"If cussing counts, yes. If not, no. For a man who's already been outed by his partner and the man he was threatening, he seems to think his silence is going to be the key to get out. After talk of Ida, he doubled down on the nothing he was giving. But we'll see how long that lasts. I've found during my time on the job that men are the ones who really love to talk."

"Let's hope for Kristine's sake he does it sooner rather than later."

Sheriff Bennet agreed with that. She'd already told Lily that the search for Kristine had been expanded. Police from the city, reserve deputies and volunteers had been activated.

It was a familiar feeling for the town.

Something the sheriff noted.

"I wonder if the fair will ever come back to Kelby Creek now," she wondered aloud. "After everything Darren McHale must have done to convince them to come back too, only to have Jacob, his own assistant, turn out to be a son of a gun."

That was news to Lily.

"Jacob Anderson worked for Darren McHale?"

"Yep. Apparently he's had the gig for upward of five years."

Lily let out a cuss. The sheriff didn't seem to mind.

"Why does someone working for a McHale try his

hand at getting into the meth business? That's like winning the lottery and then trying to start up a counterfeit money ring."

"Oh, no. Jacob was broke," the sheriff corrected. "I mean, no savings, credit cards maxed, in debt up to his eyeballs." When Lily gave her a questioning look she explained. "His wife, Gwen, told us they had gone through two failed IVF rounds in the last two years. Insurance didn't cover either and they had to pay out-of-pocket." She shook her head, disgusted. "Can you imagine going through all that only to find out that your husband of ten years was seeing a twenty-year-old?"

Lily couldn't.

"Some people make decisions that keep me up at night," she said. "I can't imagine how their loved ones feel."

The sheriff agreed and stood with a stretch. She thanked Lily for the coffee and said it was time to go.

"You earned the update," she told Lily at the front door. "But you've also earned the rest. I don't expect to talk to you until next week, okay?"

Lily nodded.

"Okay."

Sheriff Bennet walked out to her truck just as the sound of footfalls came down the stairs behind Lily.

"I was going to come out earlier but I figured you might not want a dripping-wet man in a towel to come say hi to your boss. So I decided to stay out of sight for a bit."

Ant was grinning. It made Lily's stomach fluttery again, a feeling she was starting to equate with the man.

"I'm sure Sheriff Bennet would have had a fun time with that."

They went to the kitchen together where Lily brewed him a cup of coffee. He'd had a later start to the day after finally getting some good sleep, only waking up after Lily had finished with her own shower and dressed.

Ant took the cup but didn't waste any time with his curiosity.

"Was the sheriff's visit a good one or a bad one?"

Lily led him to the dining room table. She was hesitant to answer but didn't realize why right away.

"Kristine is still missing but they found Bryant Lautner."

Ant sat up straight in his chair.

It dawned on Lily then that a part of her didn't want to tell Ant what she'd learned. That Bryant hadn't been involved in Ida's kidnapping. That her small lead that had brought him to town, to her, was now gone.

It made guilt well up in Lily.

She shouldn't have wanted to tell him because it meant that what had happened to Ida was still as unsolved as it had been fourteen years ago.

Yet the main worry she felt now was that he would leave.

Sure, they'd had a great night, but nothing between them had been set in stone.

Ant still had an apartment and life in North Carolina.

She had a life in Kelby Creek.

Neither had even broached the subject of their individual futures, never mind one that might have them together.

But she wasn't about to keep the truth from the man.

So Lily told him exactly what the sheriff had told her.

"I guess it *was* a coincidence, in a roundabout way," she added on when she was finished. "Looking into someone from an old lead at the same time they're involved in an active case. I can't say that's happened to me before."

Ant didn't say anything for a moment.

Lily let him have his thoughts.

When he met her eyes again, Lily felt heat rise in her. Something she was also starting to equate with the man.

"So, what happens next?"

Like in Kristine Cho's bedroom, it was another broad question.

This time, Lily had some answers.

"Everyone in the department is focused on looking for Kristine and trying to figure out the missing pieces between Arturo, Jacob and Bryant. Everything we've learned since finding the buried box has been passed over to Kenneth and Foster while they work together. On that front, we wait." Lily didn't like waiting; she didn't like admitting that that was the smartest play for her. It felt like giving up, even though she knew it wasn't. "As for Ida...we keep looking."

Ant nodded deep.

"I'm good with that."

He didn't ask about what that meant for him and Lily and she didn't bring it up. He did, however, have a more immediate plan.

"If you're feeling up to it, I thought we could go pay Winnie a visit," he added on. "When I dropped her off last night she seemed so...lost. I know we can't do more for her with Kris than is already being done but maybe we could keep her company for a little bit? Order in some Crisp's?"

The heat she'd been feeling around Ant became a nice warmth.

"I think that's a great idea."

They finished their coffees, grabbed their things and decided Cook should ride along. According to Ant his presence had seemed to help the young woman the other day.

Lily paused by the gun safe in her closet when grabbing her blazer.

It was over.

She was off the clock.

She didn't need her handgun.

Lily felt that helplessness she'd been staving off since finding out Kristine was missing. The same vulnerability that had made a home in her after Ida had been taken. She hesitated a beat longer before making a decision.

She shut the closet door. Then they piled into her car and drove a few streets down to Winnie's.

Lily wondered if she'd have guests, perhaps her parents or her boyfriend, after everything that had happened.

But there was no car in the drive at all.

The front door, however, was ajar.

Lily and Ant shared a look. She let him take the lead into the home.

"Winnie?" he called out. "It's Ant and Lily."

No one answered and, as far as Lily could tell, nothing was disturbed.

Wordlessly they went to the second floor and split to explore in opposite directions.

Ant went to Winnie's room, Lily to Kris's.

Once again, nothing look disturbed.

She went to the closet, opened it and saw the expensive shoes in a box. She went to the dresser, found the lingerie. The note, however, wasn't in the nightstand. Neither was the diamond ring in the vanity.

Ant filled the doorway with his broad frame. His face was solemn.

"She's not in her room. But this was on the floor next to her bed."

He held out a small piece of paper.

Compact handwriting spelled out a simple name.

"'Finnigan's,'" she read out. "Finnigan's Fun House?"

Ant wasn't pleased.

"It looks like it might be time to finally go to the fair."

Chapter Nineteen

"We've never seen the handwriting on that note before," Lily pointed out from the driver's seat. "For all we know it could be Winnie's."

She said the words and Ant heard the anxiety in them.

"The front door was left open and the number she gave us is going to voice mail," Ant returned.

Lily shifted in her seat. They were almost to the fairgrounds.

"We're also on edge," she continued. "That has to be noted."

Ant confirmed. "Definitely noted."

The rain hadn't come yet but the sky was a dark blanket of warning. The local radio station had already issued an alert for a storm expected to be on the bad side of awful. They'd even been put in a tornado watch, though that was more normal than not.

What wasn't normal was Winnie's front door being open and a note that matched one her missing roommate had been given. At least, the location.

"You said your guys looked into Finnigan's Fun House after we found Kristine's note, right?"

Lily nodded. "They even talked to the operator and he said he saw nothing out of the ordinary. He didn't recognize Kristine's picture, either."

"Then again, a lot of people go to the fair. He could be mistaken."

"True." Lily let out a long sigh. She turned them onto the dirt road that led to the parking lot in the distance.

The woods began behind that.

Normally he wouldn't talk about those woods but after the night he'd spent with Lily—after the feelings he'd shared—he didn't feel the need to censor himself.

"I hate being this close to them." His words had turned bitter.

Lily didn't need him to explain.

"Me too."

Kelby Creek might have been a small town but the fairgrounds looked like they went on forever. That included the makeshift lot, mowed down and covered in dirt, that ran the length of the main fairway behind the ticket stands. There were only a few cars in the lot where there were usually hundreds. Lily parked in the row closest to the entrance.

"I saw a post online that said today's opening was delayed for the weather but some staff and maintenance workers were asked to come in still." She shut off the engine. Cook sat up in the back seat. Ant pointed to one of the cars near them.

"That's Winnie's car," he said.

"Maybe she's here working on the clown routine." It was a statement but Lily didn't sound like she believed it. "But it can't hurt to go in and check. Come on."

They got out of the car, Cook leashed to Ant's hand, and walked fast to the ticket booth. There was a lone worker behind the Plexiglas window. He looked fresh out of high school. He also looked fresh out of patience.

"Fair's closed until the storm front passes through," he said with clear annoyance in his voice.

Lily matched his volume but put authority in her every word.

"I'm Detective Howard with the Dawn County Sheriff's Department. Have you seen this woman?" Lily pulled out her phone and in the process flashed her holstered gun and badge.

Ant hadn't realized she'd brought either with her when they'd gone to Winnie's.

He was glad for it now.

The boy sat up and dropped his phone. A game danced on the screen but his focus was all Lily.

She tapped Winnie's face in the picture they had of her and Kristine.

The boy nodded quickly.

"Yeah, she's inside. Came in a few minutes ago with some guy."

"I thought you said the fair was closed?" Lily asked.

The boy went red in the face. He got all squirmy.

"He, uh, paid me to give him a few minutes."

"And what did he look like?" Ant could feel Lily vibrating with the need to go. To do something. Cook's tail thumped him in the leg, the dog no doubt picking up on their readiness.

The boy looked perplexed by the question.

"Uh, I don't know. Older? He gave me a hundred

so I figured it was a good cause. Plus his lady looked upset so I thought why not since this place probably isn't opening until right before closing time anyway."

Lily turned to Ant.

"Older, has money to spend, Finnigan's?" Before he could comment back Lily was barking at the boy, "We're going in."

He didn't try to stop them but did call out when Lily hustled through the gate.

She didn't listen.

"Jacob and his wife were broke, doing IVF for at least two years, and married ten," she hurriedly said, matching her stride that had her, Ant and Cook making quick work of the lit-up thoroughfare. "Then suddenly he's dishing out expensive things, trying to be a meth supplier and seeing a twenty-year-old? And *then* after all of that he admits to it, says Kris is gone, and tells me to tell 'her' that he loves her. If he knew Kristine was gone, was he talking about his wife?"

"You don't think Jacob was who Kristine was having an affair with?"

"Do you? I mean, either Jacob was that good at hiding who he really was or—"

"He took the fall for who it really was."

Lily shrugged as she walked. They were almost past the food vendors' booths.

"Or he was blackmailed? His family threatened maybe?"

"So, what, you think that Winnie could be with Kristine's real mystery guy?"

Lily gave him a slightly exasperated look.

"Weren't you the one who wanted us to bolt out here because you were worried that something was going on with Winnie?"

He wasn't going to deny it. He was going to go to the next logical question.

"If she is here with him, then does that mean she's been in on it or she's the next victim?"

"Let's find her first. I haven't been here in so long. Do you know where Finnigan's is?"

Ant did know but only because the fair hardly ever changed. The fun house, house of mirrors and horror motel were all in a line on the west side of the fair. He led the way, Cook jogging along to keep up at his side, when after passing the Tilt-A-Whirl he finally saw the two-story attraction and its bright red-and-orange sign.

"The bottom floor has your standard fun house tricks and in the back you can take the stairs up to the second floor, which has the black light room," Ant said. "There's usually an operator at the side there but it looks like—"

A woman screamed, interrupting him.

Lily was off, her gun out, within a second. Ant only made it past her because he had longer legs and no broken ribs. He bounded up the first metal stairs and jumped the gate made for the line. He was inside the first floor, running past the moving mirrors, sliding floors and rotating tunnel. Ant was grateful they were all turned off. He was also grateful the house hadn't changed since he was a teenager.

The back stairs were right where he remembered.

He took them two at a time and spun around into the main section of the second floor.

The moving parts weren't on downstairs but up here the black lights were.

Ant's surroundings were bathed in bright shades of neon.

So was the man holding Winnie in the middle of the room.

"Hey!" Ant's yell came out only a second before he had his hands on the back of the man's shirt. He yanked him away from Winnie in a move that worked every arm muscle he had.

Lily was right behind him, yelling out an identification and showing her weapon.

The man didn't fight back.

He looked confused.

So was Ant when he heard Winnie yelling, too.

"Stop! Let him go!"

THE BLACK LIGHT room turned to normal again as Winnie flipped a switch in the corner. Her eyes were swollen but it didn't look like she was currently crying.

"That's my boyfriend," she added, pointing to the man that Ant had thrown almost clear across the room.

Now with better lighting Lily recognized the EMT who'd helped her a few days ago. Colton, in street clothes, looked slightly terrified.

Ant, still huffing from adrenaline most likely, gave Winnie what Lily could only describe as a big brother tone.

"We heard you scream!"

Winnie pointed to a dip in the floor at the front of the room.

"I tripped. Colton just picked me up."

Lily lowered her weapon.

"We went by your house to check on you," she explained. "Your front door was open and a note that said 'Finnigan's' was on your floor."

If Winnie was offended at her privacy being invaded, she didn't say so. Instead she gave Colton a confused glance. Despite having just gotten himself off the floor, he looked sheepish.

"I was talking to my partner and he was going on and on about next week's schedule and I must have spaced on locking up. I'm sorry." Colton looked to Lily. "The front door latch sometimes doesn't catch."

"And the note?" Ant still sounded hot. He'd been ready to defend Winnie and have to fight for her. His fists were still at his sides.

Colton gave Winnie a confused look this time. She returned it then answered Lily.

"I don't know about a note."

Lily and Ant turned to each other, equally perplexed.

"Then why are you two here? At Finnigan's?" Lily asked.

Colton spoke up.

"After everything that's happened I wanted to try and cheer Winnie up," he said. "I knew she didn't want to be around a lot of people so I thought I'd take her to her favorite ride when no one was here. I paid the ticket guy up front for five minutes."

"You paid him one hundred dollars for five minutes?" Ant asked.

Winnie looked startled at that.

"You paid him a hundred dollars?"

Colton answered them both with a nod.

"I just wanted to give her some happiness, even if it was only for a few minutes."

Winnie melted into a smile, a look that was reflected on Colton's face.

Lily holstered her gun. They were just two people in love trying to grab on to something happy during a troubling time.

Lily understood the urge.

The impulse.

She glanced at Ant, who was already looking at her.

That heat, that flutter, both came back with a vengeance.

Lily cleared her throat.

She wasn't the only one.

Ant made little work of the space between them as a new figure entered the room.

An intimidatingly tall man, in a button-down shirt, dark jeans and loafers. He had brown hair slicked back and Cook on a leash at his side.

Lily hooked her hand around Ant's elbow to stop him from advancing on the man.

They'd already busted in on a couple's innocent fun, it would be a shame to bust up a McHale.

"Mr. McHale," Lily called out. The older man looked as startled as Ant when he finally made the connection.

He stopped in his tracks.

Darren McHale wasn't as widely popular as his older brother and sister-in-law. He had nowhere near his niece Annie's fame. The news stories, tabloids, online conspiracy theories and even locals often forgot his name. That was if they ever knew he existed at all. He had money, sure, but he'd never spent it as publicly or as charitably as his family.

The only thing of note he'd done since Annie's kidnapping and then her parents leaving town was to take up residence in their old home. The rumor was that he'd stayed in case Annie came back so that his brother and sister-in-law could leave without guilt, and grieve and heal in peace somewhere.

Lily wasn't sure if that was true but she felt pity for the man.

He ran his own lumber business, was unmarried, had had a falling-out with his son and lived in a town that mourned his niece more than it ever recognized that he was still with them.

Ant had told Lily she wasn't some ghost.

She felt like that wasn't true for Darren.

Even the smile in greeting he gave them looked off.

"I'm sorry if I scared you, I—I heard yelling." He motioned to Cook, who licked at his hand. "And then I saw this guy outside."

"That would be my bad." Ant reached out for the leash and Cook happily changed sides. "We thought Winnie was in trouble so I just ran."

Darren surveyed the room. Lily felt another blush, though this one was more professional.

"Mr. McHale, I'm Detective Howard with the sheriff's department and this is Anthony Perez. We had cause to worry that our friend Winnie here was in danger and we came to check it out." Lily gave a little laugh. "Turns out all we did was interrupt a date and we were just figuring that out."

Darren's eyebrows scrunched together.

One of the pitfalls of not knowing much about Darren McHale was not knowing his manner. Did he think this was funny? Or was he about to raise hell?

Lily wanted to bypass finding out.

Plus, since he was there, she might as well ask him some questions that were now burning a hole in her about Jacob Anderson.

"Now that you're here though, this works out," she hurriedly tacked on. "I was actually wondering if I could ask you a few questions?"

Lily couldn't read the man's expression right away. She worried she'd crossed a line while off duty. Yet a warm enough smile spread across his lips after a moment.

"I have a few things I need to do before the storm rolls in but if you don't mind walking and talking while I do them, I don't mind, either." He looked at the other three adults. "But I'm afraid you all can't stay in the fun house. Not unattended. It's a liability issue."

Colton was the first to comply. Probably since he'd been the first to break the rules. He led the way back outside. The sky overhead seemed to have darkened even more. It felt like night.

"I have a few things to do in the back office," Darren reiterated. "I can talk to you on the way."

There was an emphasis on the word *you*. Lily picked up on it. So did Ant.

"I'll walk them out," he said, indicating Colton and Winnie. "Cook and I will stay by the car."

Lily mouthed her thanks, then turned to her new companion. "I'm ready when you are."

Darren McHale smiled again.

If Lily had known what the next hour would bring, she would have grabbed Ant's hand and never let go.

But she hadn't known.

None of them had.

Chapter Twenty

"Jacob was a good man, but isn't that how it always starts?"

Darren McHale was walking at a brisk pace but his tone was the opposite of energetic. He sounded tired. A man who knew of tragedy. A man who knew that anyone could become a monster.

"I originally hired him as my assistant because of his attention to detail, his drive to get the job done and, to be frank, his utter disinterest in gossip," Darren continued. "Spreading it, listening to it, trying to find more to add to it. As you can probably guess, that's a quality I've come to deeply appreciate, especially after what happened with my niece."

Lily hadn't expected him to mention Annie McHale at all. She decided to show him that she wasn't here for anything other than what he knew about their current case.

"So you had no idea, no suspicion of him?" she asked. "He wasn't acting odd or changing up his work habits?"

Darren shook his head. They walked past the teacups that she'd almost thrown up on while riding with her father when she was a kid. It felt like an odd juxtaposition to their situation now.

"No. I had no idea," he answered. "Whatever stress or concern I felt from him I counted it toward his and Gwen's attempts to get pregnant. When Sheriff Bennet visited me last night I had to ask her three times if she was sure it was him."

Lily didn't mean to but she imagined Jacob's last moments with a stomach-turning vividness.

"It was Jacob all right."

Darren slowed a little.

"I heard what you went through with him. I truly am sorry. That had to be hard, especially with what you've already been through."

They turned by the Ferris wheel while a crack of thunder sounded in the distance. The entire fair was lit up around them but absent of any workers or staff. A ghost town for two haunted souls.

Lily hoped the rain would hold off while her haunted self finished her impromptu interview.

"The last week definitely hasn't been the best," she concluded. "I'm still standing though and I'm grateful for that."

Darren smiled.

"While I agree your week has probably been a little wild compared to what it is normally, I was referring to what happened when you were a teen."

They slowed and turned off to follow a gravel path to the back office. The building was half office, half warehouse. It was the only structure that was permanent on the fairgrounds, even when the fair wasn't in town. She'd been in there once before.

Lily gave him a questioning look.

"When I was a teen?" She knew he meant what happened to Ida, but still, she wanted him to clarify. Once she'd become an adult Lily could count on one hand how many people had mentioned what happened to her back then.

"The abduction of Miss Ida Perez," he confirmed.

Lily kept her question on her face.

He gave her another apologetic look.

"When your niece's abduction makes national news and is still unsolved, you become familiar with all the unsolved abductions in the area," he explained. "Though, to be honest, I remember Miss Perez's case from the news. It's also a memory that sticks considering my son Parker and I had our falling-out a few weeks later. He's always been against this town. One of his former classmates being taken was just the excuse he needed to finally leave."

He opened the side door with one of his keys. It led into the warehouse portion of the building. The space was expansive, cold, and partially filled with boxes, tools and miscellaneous parts from rides and attractions. He waved his hand to the opposite side of the room where the offices were.

Lily had already known that he and his son were estranged but she hadn't known the reason Parker had left.

"I had no idea he left because of what happened to Ida."

Darren let out a tired laugh.

"That and my overbearing parenting apparently," he said. "His mother, rest her soul, was the one with the soft touch and kind words. According to him, I was wanting in that area. I'm not sure I blame him for leaving, though. We both know that this town takes more than it ever gives."

Lily knew he was right. He kept on to drive his point home.

"Ida should have had a full, happy life. Just as sweet Annie, Kristine and Claudia should have had. The same for Jacob and his wife."

Lily ran names in her memory.

"Claudia?"

Darren slowed. It put them halfway through the warehouse. Another crack of thunder sounded. This time it was closer.

"A young woman who was taken from the next county around the same time Miss Perez was."

Lily shook her head.

"I don't remember hearing about that one." Lily knew she wasn't an expert in many things but one investigation she knew inside and out was Ida's. There had been no abduction in the entire state of Alabama for two weeks before and after Ida's. The next person to be taken was a child in north Alabama by his father, later returned safely to his mother. There was no Claudia.

Darren looked thoughtful.

"I suppose I'm misremembering, then." He sighed. "Sometimes it's hard to keep all of Kelby Creek's tragedies in line."

Lily would have normally given that to him but a

nagging feeling had been woken up within her. She didn't know why but that brought her right back to Bryant Lautner.

"Speaking of tragedies, what do you know about Bryant Lautner?" she asked. "He's around your age and Kelby Creek's so small. You must have known him when you were younger?"

Darren shook his head.

They were almost to the door now.

"The only thing I really remember about that man when we were younger was this awful flu he gave me when he was setting up his mother's memorial service with my sister-in-law's help," he said. "It was so rough I coughed up blood at one point. It was probably the worst I've ever felt."

Lily didn't realize it but she'd already stopped walking.

The switch she normally threw to keep her emotions out of the equation had just been yanked off the wall.

There was no way.

No way she'd heard him right.

He couldn't have been...

Was he?

Lily's mind filled to the brim with questions.

Yet, she focused on the memory from the woods.

The sound of a man coughing.

After all of these years, after everything she'd gone through to get to the moment of being with the man in the woods...

Was she finally there?

One look back at Darren and whatever emotion was on her face was enough to stop him in his tracks.

She knew then.

And he knew that she knew.

For a second, all they did was stare at one another.

In the next, he sighed again.

"You know, I always wondered if you heard me coughing that night." He shrugged. "I guess now I know."

Lily pulled her gun out and shot just as Darren side-stepped.

He yelled out in pain as the bullet grazed his arm but it didn't stop him from launching himself at her.

Adrenaline hadn't yet poured through her and pushed out the pain in her rib cage. She tried to avoid the force of his body weight but all she did was catch it with the left side of her body instead of head-on.

They both went down.

The air was knocked clear from Lily's lungs but Darren wasn't faring much better. Blood from his arm dripped onto her as Lily tried to bring up her gun. Darren huffed and puffed trying to straddle her but moved his attention to her weapon. He managed to use one hand to slam her wrist against the concrete floor. Lily knew her gun was coming loose so she did the only thing she could.

She flung it away from both of them then yanked her knee up to his groin.

Darren yelled out as Lily bucked him off.

The second his weight was off her, she scrambled toward her gun.

As she grabbed it she was already imagining shooting the man in the leg to disable him.

However, he said the only thing in the world that would stop her.

"Put the gun down or she dies!"

Lily spun around and froze her trigger finger.

There was a good amount of distance between them now but Lily could see his face clearly.

"Who?" Lily yelled. Her voice was hoarse. The hit to the floor had been harder than she'd thought.

Darren had his hands up. His answer was too strong. Too confident.

"Kristine Cho is in a box somewhere in this town, suffocating because you showed up here. Because you interrupted me."

Lily shook her gun.

"I don't believe you."

Darren pointed to the door they'd been about to walk through. Next to it was a shovel.

"I was about to go get her since she's been in that box since last night. Bryant was supposed to get her but he never showed."

Lily had some decisions to make.

The first was to believe him or not.

"Why?"

"Because that's where we keep them until we move them."

Lily's stomach plummeted.

"Them?"

"The girls," he yelled back. "And *that* girl is going

to die if you don't put down your gun." Lily hesitated.
But only for a moment.

She had no choice but to believe him.

"Where is she?"

"Put the gun and your phone down and I'll tell you.
If she's not already out of air, you can save her."

Lily knew her next decision was the most crucial.

It could be the difference between her life and Kristine's.

It could be the difference between catching Darren McHale or letting him use his money to disappear.

There was no way to know until she decided.

So Lily chose Kristine, hoping he wasn't lying.

But she wasn't about to give in to him fully.

She took the clip out of her gun and put it in her pocket. She threw the rest of the gun across the floor toward the door they'd come in. Her phone went next.

Then she aimed her righteous anger at Darren McHale.

"Tell me where she is!"

If the urgency hadn't been so great, she might have closed the distance between them and slugged him at how he flashed a quick smile.

"The last place you and Anthony Perez would ever look."

Lily's veins were now completely flooded with adrenaline.

She knew where Kristine was.

And Darren knew that.

"I'd be running if I were you," he warned.

Lily didn't stop to think her next move through.

She ran to the door and grabbed the shovel.

Then she was outside, opening the back gate and running into the woods with an awful sense of déjà vu.

ANT WATCHED COLTON and Winnie drive off. He'd apologized again for messing up their date, then he'd given the EMT a piece of his mind about making sure to lock his girlfriend's doors.

After that he'd leaned against Lily's car with Cook at his side.

He was mulling over what Lily had said about Jacob not being Kristine's secret boyfriend when he heard the gunshot.

Cook barked, just as Ant took off.

"Call the cops!" he yelled to the boy in the ticket stand.

Ant made fast work of running through the thoroughfare and even faster work of finding the office at the back of the fairgrounds. He heard nothing on the way to the building. Only his footfalls and Cook's panting as he followed.

He wasn't sure if that was a good thing or not.

The door closest to him was open.

"Lily!"

His voice echoed through the warehouse.

He stopped when he saw her gun on the floor ahead of him. Her phone next to it.

Ant grabbed the gun and redirected his attention to the opposite side of the room. He saw another door, open and streaked with blood.

He didn't wait around.

Ant ran full tilt toward and through it.

He was in an office. He scanned the room and his eyes lit on a back door that had blood smeared across the handle.

Ant pushed out into the darkness just in time to see a man go into the tree line in the distance.

It was without a doubt Darren McHale.

The shotgun he was holding was also unmistakable.

Ant didn't yell for Lily this time.

If Lily was being chased and without a weapon, she was going somewhere she knew better than her attacker.

Ant tried to make as little noise as he could running into the woods. Cook was still with him, running hard, about ten to twelve feet behind Darren. If the dog could ambush the man, Ant could save Lily.

A plan made harder by the fact that the gun in his hand didn't have a clip.

Still, he could use it as a blunt object. If not, he'd make sure his fists would do the trick.

Thunder boomed overhead.

Ant could barely see between the trees.

He moved fast despite his vision.

His childhood home was on the other side of the woods. Somewhere between him and it was the creek. Between it and him was Lily, unarmed and possibly hurt. Between her and Ant was a man with a shotgun.

A nearly overwhelming sense of helplessness rammed into Ant's chest.

The last time he'd been in these woods, he'd lost someone he loved.

He refused to do that again.

Chapter Twenty-One

The rain started falling just as Lily heard the creek in the distance. Before that she'd heard someone behind her.

Darren McHale had let her go knowing his secret.

There was no doubt in her mind that he would follow her into the woods and try to keep that secret from ever leaving it.

Yet Lily had believed him about Kristine so she'd done the only two things she could in the situation.

She'd run as fast as she'd ever run and then thrown herself behind a tree to hide.

She had to figure Darren had a weapon. One he would use on Lily fast once he caught her.

So she held her breath and planned to catch him first. She hadn't strayed from running the most direct path to the creek and neither had Darren. It was almost too easy to pinpoint where he was going to be.

Lily jumped out, bent low and swung the shovel like all of Wrigley Field was watching her.

She was right on the money.

The metal part of the shovel connected with Darren's legs. His momentum and sheer size sent Lily to her backside just as he yelled out and fell a few feet from her.

Lily was also right about the man having a weapon. She spied the shotgun as it flew from his hands.

Lily struggled to stand, tightening her grip on the shovel, as Darren rolled around in the dirt, feeling for the gun.

He found it but Lily was quicker with the shovel. She swung it like a golf club.

The metal head connected with a sickening thud beneath Darren's chin.

He dropped his gun, then the rest of his body went limp, falling to the dirt in a heap.

Lily was breathing hard. Adrenaline had her heart beating so fast it felt like it was about to tear out of her body.

She couldn't imagine how Kristine felt.

Lily bent down, grabbed the shotgun and ran with it and the shovel past the unconscious man.

The sound of the creek grew louder.

The trees started to thin into a clearing.

The clearing…

Lily slowed, but only for a moment.

She was standing where Darren had been all those years ago. She looked over to the water.

Where Ant had been.

Then she looked at the expanse of ground beyond the water.

Where she had been when she'd had to decide whether to save Ant or Ida.

Lily had been at that spot, at that creek, in the same woods, for years.

With startling clarity she realized she had never left.

She'd been trapped in this spot in Kelby Creek since she was seventeen.

Ant was wrong.

She was a ghost and *this* was where she haunted.

You know this place, she told herself. *You know what's different.*

Lily took the smallest of breaths.

With her eyes she traced the ground again, the water, the trees the deputies' flashlight beams had bounced across when they'd hurried out to them.

Lily stopped.

One of the trees was gone. The one with the knot that used to be as big as her hand.

The dirt where it should have been was disturbed.

Lily splashed across the water. She dropped the shotgun when she reached the fresh dirt and sank the shovel into the earth. The dirt she brought back she tossed over her shoulder. On the second stab into the ground, she hit something hard.

It timed poorly with someone crashing through the trees behind her.

Lily spun around. She must have been hurting more than she thought, because she lost her balance and hit the ground.

It was only good fortune that the man who appeared wasn't Darren McHale.

"Lily!"

Ant made it across the water without stopping. Cook was on his heels.

She could have cried, if there'd been time.

Instead, she got back up and pointed her shovel back down at the hole.

"Kristine is inside!"

Ant didn't need more of an explanation.

He took the shovel and drove it deep into the ground. He hit the top of the box and readjusted his aim. Dirt flew over his shoulder, and Lily dropped to her knees to help dig with her hands.

"It was Darren," Lily cried out. Tears of anger and exhaustion and pain were starting to burn her eyes. "Ant, he was there that night. He took Ida."

Ant didn't pause.

He didn't stop.

He kept digging.

The top of the box was fully uncovered within seconds. Ant started to move the dirt to get to the side just as they had the first night he came to town.

This time there was no recording of Annie McHale.

There was, however, a voice.

It was faint.

It was Kristine.

As Lily yelled out to her, urging her to hold on, she barely heard the splashing behind them.

Ant shouted for Lily's attention but not in time.

Darren lunged at her.

Ant managed to push her out of the way of the man but Lily still felt like a fool for not keeping the shotgun in her hands.

Terror consumed her as Darren took it back into his.

Ant was quicker with his reflexes. Just as he'd done at Bryant Lautner's workshop he ran Lily into the trees, this time dragging her.

She looked over her shoulder to see Darren cock the gun.

Ant used his strength to sling her along with him behind one of the trees. Shotgun pellets bit into the bark on the other side.

Ant wasn't done moving. He handed something to Lily so fast it took her a beat to figure out it was her gun.

She might have dropped the ball with the shotgun but at least she'd kept her clip.

Darren shot again. With his arms and body Ant made a cage around her but gave her the space she needed to load the gun.

In one fluid movement, he pulled back and Lily rolled to the side, her gun up and ready.

She couldn't see Darren all that well but he must have seen her enough to know that running for cover might be the best idea.

She caught the barest hint of movement and swung her weapon to the side, and fired.

Darren yelled out and she saw him then as he grasped his leg. She'd wounded him. He retreated across the creek. Lily tried to get another shot off but her aim wasn't there.

Ant pulled her to him. She met his eyes.

The world around them became fourteen years younger.

Ant's hair was dark and wet against his face. His eyes matched the sky, stormy and fierce. He was determined.

This time, though, he was Lily.

Seventeen, terrified, long hair tangled from the rain.

At a crossroad.

Two choices and one decision to make that could change everything.

He could save the person who needed rescuing or he could go after Ida's kidnapper.

In that moment, Lily understood that in between the softness of her sheets back home Ant had been right all along.

"There is no choice," she said. "Save the one you can."

As Ant picked up the shovel, Lily turned and ran. Ant didn't stop her.

She ran across the dirt and through the creek water, pushing past every inch of pain. Darren hadn't expected her to fight back. He hadn't expected her at all. That was more than apparent as she spotted him doubling back toward the fair. He had no plan.

And he had terrible aim.

He spun around and shot off to the side of her once. Then tried again.

That shot had Lily move for cover.

She didn't stay there long.

Lily stepped out and fired her weapon again.

Darren yelled out.

This time, he fell.

Lily was on him in a second. She picked up his discarded shotgun and trained both weapons on him.

He was in bad shape, slumped on his side.

He met her gaze and coughed through a laugh.

"They—they'll never believe you. I'm—I'm a McHale."

Lily shook her head.

"The only reason you got away from us the first time was because we were kids," she bit out. "We're not kids anymore."

Lily holstered her gun. She took the butt of the shotgun and brought it down on the man's head.

This time when he went limp, she knew he wouldn't be getting up anytime soon.

She turned and ran back to the creek.

The shovel was next to Ant. So was a piece of the box. In his arms was a young woman. Lily dropped next to them both to help pull her all the way out.

Ant held Kristine Cho as she looked up at Lily.

"Hi, Kris, we've been looking for you."

Kristine's voice was weak. "I'm glad you found me."

Lily reached out and touched Ant's shoulder.

She gave it a squeeze.

He met her eye and she knew that he knew.

Ant let out a long breath.

And just like that the ghost that haunted the woods moved on.

Two days later

THE FAIR LEFT.

The media, however, still swarmed.

Darren McHale, a part of the most beloved family in Kelby Creek, had turned out to be a devil in sheep's clothing. A villain none of them had seen coming. A monster.

No one knew yet what Darren's plan had been or the level of his involvement but by his own admission, he'd been the one to take Ida.

He'd been the man in the woods.

Ant wanted answers now that the authorities had him in custody.

But a lot of things had to happen first.

Darren had to have several surgeries, for starters. He'd had two bullet wounds, a graze, a busted knee and a broken jaw. All of which were from Lily. Something that made Ant insanely proud.

It had made Lily feel a certain type of way, too.

Later that night in her bed, she'd told Ant that it had felt vindicating to finally catch him.

He'd agreed because it was true.

Still, a part of him hurt for Ida.

What had happened to his sister?

It was a question that didn't get answered right away.

After that they'd had to wait a day for Kristine to recover enough to talk. She'd been dehydrated and close to suffocating. The doctors guessed another few minutes and she wouldn't have made it out alive. When she was able, she asked for Lily and Ant to come into her room. She was weak but she grabbed their hands and held on to them. They all stood that way for a minute before giving her space to rest.

Then Ant put on a nice shirt and jeans, helped Lily do the same since her ribs were still bruised and broken, and they headed to the department to get some clarity on everything that happened. No one batted an eye when Cook came in with them.

The dog sat down between Lily and Ant as they settled into the conference room. Detective Gray was the only one currently inside.

"Sorry we've been a bit quiet on our side of things over the last day or so," he told them. "We've had a lot of new discoveries, and piecing together all of it has been a not-so-small task."

Lily gave the man a questioning look.

Ant voiced it.

"Does that mean we know what all happened now?"

Kenneth nodded.

"Thanks to you two, Bryant striking a deal to talk, Kristine Cho's account of what happened, and a few other sources, we do." He referred to his notes only once before continuing.

"Fourteen years ago Bryant and Darren struck up a friendship after Darren's wife passed from cancer. Bryant's mother was also fighting it and was running out of money fast for the treatment. When he approached Darren about borrowing some, Darren revealed that he wasn't exactly as wealthy as his brother. So they asked for money from Annie's parents and were turned down. Bryant's mother passed shortly after anyway but Darren and his friendship stuck. Instead of moving on, they became angry. Bitter. Bryant said that Darren equated all of his problems to not having enough money and spoke to his brother about it. He was given a handout to start his own business but he blew the money. When he needed more, he was cut off. So he and Bryant met a man who gave them a different suggestion for bringing in the big bucks."

Kenneth gave Ant a quick look. One that let Ant know he wasn't going to like what was said next.

Lily's hand found his under the table before Kenneth continued.

"They got into human trafficking and hid behind the McHale brand of fame to do it in relative secret." Ant gritted his teeth. Lily squeezed his hand. "We can't tell if they were good at it or bad. There's some information we're still getting to let us know which. But they did appear to stop for several years and we think we know why."

Kenneth slid a picture across the table.

It was a McHale family Christmas card. Ant recognized some of them but not the young man Kenneth pointed to.

"That's Parker McHale," Kenneth explained.

"Darren's son?" Lily asked.

Kenneth nodded.

"He left the family home when he was younger and has stayed out of the spotlight since. The only time he surfaced was when the FBI deep dove into the family after Annie went missing. He was, at the time, living in Tennessee on a ranch with his partner and their child. Soon after that they moved again, back off everyone's radar. We're still waiting to talk to him now."

"But what does this have to do with Ida?" Ant

couldn't help but ask. "And Kristine? Was he in on it with his dad?"

Kenneth shook his head.

"We've been led to believe that he actually fled town because he knew what his father was capable of."

Kenneth shifted in his chair and Ant detected a change in his demeanor. He looked Ant right in the eye, resolute and solemn.

"From what we've been told, Ida and Parker were secretly dating at the time of her abduction and the *reason* she was taken was because she overheard Darren and Bryant planning another attempt. They found out and before she could tell anyone, she was taken."

Ant shook his head. He couldn't focus on the secret relationship because his mind went right back to the day of Ida's abduction.

"That's why she was so upset," he realized. "We were out in the yard... She'd just gotten home and I was trying to get her to tell me what was wrong. But she never did because...that's when she was taken."

Kenneth nodded.

"Bryant said Darren panicked and grabbed her."

Ant was seeing red.

"Did he say what he did to her?" He could barely get the question out.

"No. Neither man did."

Ant wanted to leave then. To go outside and yell. Yet Lily's hand had him stay.

Ida wasn't the only young woman in the story.

Kenneth seemed to realize this was his only opening to finish.

"After Ida's abduction they finished their planned job with Claudia Rikton. She was pronounced a runaway back then but now the FBI is looking into one of the names Bryant provided that he and Darren sold her to. After Claudia, though, they both stopped. They had a substantial amount of money from their trafficking. But it ran out recently. They were starting back up and trying to come up with a different plan to move women."

"By putting them in boxes," Lily guessed.

He nodded.

"They put boxes in several locations with the recorders and were testing out if they could remove them without arousing suspicion, even if the women made a fuss. That's what Arturo was hired for and what he was doing when he was interrupted by you two."

"So the meth lab and Jacob having an affair with Kristine was just them trying to cover it all up?" Lily asked.

Kenneth nodded again.

"Arturo wasn't supposed to get caught so when he did, Bryant said Darren became enraged, threatening to kill Bryant if he didn't figure out how to fix it. Apparently neither man accounted for you two. Since we've had a few meth labs pop up here and there, Bryant thought making Arturo's hideout look like one so when he burned the evidence no one would think anything other than a lab explosion. They also didn't account for Kristine getting suspicious of her secret boyfriend."

Darren McHale.

That had been a shock among shocks when Kris had admitted to them that it was the McHale she'd been seeing. Jacob Anderson had taken the fall for it, even going as far to help plant the evidence against him.

"Kristine confronted Darren after he lied about where he'd been during the meth lab fire and he decided to use her as the first test for their new box trick," Kenneth continued. "Since you two were back, he used the spot he'd created out there."

Lily was disgusted.

"Because it was the last place we would look. He told me that."

Ant grumbled. His anger was escalating once again.

"What about Jacob?" Lily followed up. "Why did he agree to take the fall?"

Kenneth was somber when he replied.

"He walked in on Bryant making the recordings off of Darren's computer one day when he was working. Jacob immediately went to Darren to let him know Bryant was messing around on his computer, thinking he was doing the right thing."

"'I didn't know he had a partner,'" Lily said. "That's what Jacob kept saying. He wasn't talking about Arturo and Bryant. He was talking about Bryant and Darren."

"Bryant said that Darren and Jacob had a long talk but he didn't know how Jacob was threatened to take the fall. He guessed it was something that involved his wife, Gwen. Something that spooked him enough to fully commit to Darren's orders."

"It must have been a terrifying threat for him to take his life," Ant added. "One he believed Darren would carry out if he didn't follow the plan."

Kenneth was fast with a response they all knew to be true.

"We're still trying to figure out what that threat was but only Darren and Jacob knew. The name McHale carries a lot of weight in this town. Apparently that weight can be used for awful things."

They all quieted at that.

Lily broke the silence after a moment.

"Then there's the whole question of why Darren McHale had a potentially clear recording of Annie's video on his computer," Kenneth continued. "That's currently unsolved at the moment but something we're looking into. It might just take some time."

Lily nodded, so did Ant.

"So that answers all of my questions but one," she said.

Kenneth's eyebrow raised.

"What is that?"

Lily leaned forward.

"How do you know so much about what Parker McHale did if you haven't actually talked to him yet?"

Kenneth didn't answer at first. He stood, and Ant could have sworn he saw a small smile pass over the man's lips.

"Because his partner and their child came forward as soon as the news went out that Darren McHale had been caught."

Kenneth went to the door. He opened it and stepped aside.

After a moment a preteen boy came in, tall and dark-haired. He looked familiar but Ant couldn't place him.

When his mother walked in, Ant had no trouble at all recognizing her.

Ida was older but the moment she said his name all he saw was the sixteen-year-old girl he'd been missing for fourteen years.

Epilogue

Six months later

"Listen, I know it's too soon but maybe we can just take a gander at some dresses tomorrow?"

Winnie was giving her a look that Lily had come to understand meant that Winnie had already planned their shopping expedition. Beside her, Colton wore an expression that told Lily it was a lost cause to fight his girlfriend. Still, Lily was trying to be practical.

"Winnie, we're in the middle of my engagement party. For an engagement that happened less than two days ago. Maybe we should hold off on wedding dress shopping for at least a week?"

Winnie made an exasperated sound. She threw up her hands, turned to Kristine across the decorated backyard and shook her head.

Kris was dramatic with her disappointment. It made her date laugh.

"Fine. I'll let you catch your breath, I guess," Winnie said. She lowered her voice. "But you better believe I'm not the only one who's going to pressure you tonight."

She nodded, not so inconspicuously, to the patio. "You best believe those two are coming for you next."

Lily looked over to see that Kristine hadn't been the only one watching them. Ida and Juliet pretended, at least, to be disinterested in her.

Ida's big brother, however, feigned no such thing.

He entered the conversation by picking Lily up and spinning her into a kiss.

When her feet were on the ground again, he excused them both.

"They bothering you about the wedding already?" he asked, laughing before she could answer.

"Yes! Wedding dress shopping tomorrow, never mind that I have work."

Ant laughed again.

"You can't blame them. After the wedding you pulled off for Ida and Parker, everyone wants to return the favor."

Even after six months, the way Ant said Ida's name still made Lily's heart melt a little. The two syllables were filled with love and a gratefulness that she felt in her bones. Knowing that Ida's kidnapper was in prison for life was nothing compared to the feeling of seeing her alive and happy.

Though that had taken some time on both their parts.

True, Ant had been beside himself at seeing his sister after fourteen years. Those fourteen years of her staying in hiding had hit him hard. Especially when they found out that the day after Ida had been taken, she'd been freed.

"I was in Hunstville, in a trunk, and then suddenly

Parker was there," she'd explained to them. "He figured out where his father's partner was and managed to help me escape. We hid, wanting to make sure we had enough to take Darren down. But then we found out I was pregnant with Beau and, well, Parker knew about all the corruption already running through the town. So we decided to hide for a while." Ida had cried then as she'd looked at Ant. "I almost reached out to you a dozen times but I was so worried that they'd find a way to hurt Beau. And then, you moved and I almost reached out but The Flood happened and we didn't know who to trust."

Ida had been all-out sobbing then.

"Then we saw the news that Darren had been caught and I—I just knew in my bones that you were the one who'd done it."

In the darkness of their bedroom, Ant had admitted to Lily one night that while he would have made a different decision, he couldn't fault Ida and Parker for theirs.

"Being a McHale carries a certain weight with locals." He'd paraphrased Kenneth. "I guess that goes double for fear."

He wasn't wrong. Parker's reemergence and his father's arrest had brought the McHales right back into the spotlight.

And, for the first time, not as the victims.

But that was a whole new set of questions for another time.

Right now Lily was making sure to be in the moment with the man she loved and the man who loved her back enough to ask her to marry him. It had happened late one night while they were trying to be witches on her bed.

"Close your eyes," he'd said. "Now move that power from your belly to your hands, since we all know your head doesn't need it."

Lily had laughed but followed directions.

"I'd watch out if I were you," she'd responded. "If my hands get too much power they might just smack that cute mouth of yours."

"Then it's probably not a good idea to give them any more power, huh?"

She'd felt the bed move a second before she felt the ring on her finger.

When she'd opened her eyes, he'd told her to lie back down.

"Now, we're going to close our eyes and make some decisions," he'd said, repeating his words from the first time they'd done the exercise.

She hadn't said it then but there was never really any choice to make at all.

It had always been Ant.

Instead, in the moment, she'd just said yes.

Now they were surrounded by loved ones and celebrating each other after what had been a long fourteen years.

"You know, once Mom finishes moving in down the road and your parents head back here—not to mention Ida, Parker and Beau in the same neighborhood *and* Winnie and Kristine too—we're probably never going to be alone again."

Ant wrapped his arms around her and kissed her neck.

They both looked out at the party of people. Family, friends and colleagues.

He was right.

Lily relaxed against him.

Before Ant came back to town, Lily would have hated the thought.

Now, though, everything was different.

Now she didn't want to be alone anymore.

"Sounds good to me."

* * * * *

Look for the conclusion of Tyler Anne Snell's
The Saving Kelby Creek series when
Retracing the Investigation *goes on sale next month.*

And if you missed the previous books in the series,
look for:

Uncovering Small Town Secrets
Searching for Evidence
Surviving the Truth
Accidental Amnesia

You'll find them wherever Harlequin Intrigue
books are sold!

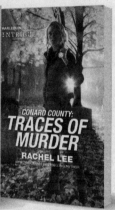

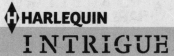

#2079 SHERIFF IN THE SADDLE
The Law in Lubbock County • by Delores Fossen
The town wants her to arrest her former boyfriend, bad boy Cullen Brodie, for a murder on his ranch—but Sheriff Leigh Mercer has no evidence and refuses. The search for the killer draws them passionately close again...and into relentless danger. Not only could Leigh lose her job for not collaring Brodie...but they could both lose their lives.

#2080 ALPHA TRACKER
K-9s on Patrol • by Cindi Myers
After lawman Dillon Diaz spent one incredible weekend with the mysterious Roslyn Kern, he's shocked to encounter her months later when he's assigned to rescue an injured hiker in the mountains. Now, battling a fiery blaze and an escaped fugitive, it's up to Dillon and his K-9, Bentley, to protect long-lost Rosie— and Dillon's unborn child.

#2081 EYEWITNESS MAN AND WIFE
A Ree and Quint Novel • by Barb Han
Relentless ATF agent Quint Casey won't let his best lead die with a murdered perp. He and his undercover wife, Agent Ree Sheppard, must secretly home in on a powerful weapons kingpin. But their undeniable attraction is breaking too many rules for them to play this mission safe—or guarantee their survival...

#2082 CLOSING IN ON THE COWBOY
Kings of Coyote Creek • by Carla Cassidy
Rancher Johnny King thought he'd moved on since Chelsea Black broke their engagement and shattered his heart. But with his emotions still raw following his father's murder, Chelsea's return to town and vulnerability touches Johnny's heart. And when a mysterious stalker threatens Chelsea's life, protecting her means risking his heart again for the woman who abandoned him.

#2083 RETRACING THE INVESTIGATION
The Saving Kelby Creek Series • by Tyler Anne Snell
When Sheriff Jones Murphy rescues his daughter and her teacher, the widower is surprised to encounter Cassandra West again—and there's no mistaking she's pregnant. Now someone wants her dead for unleashing a secret that stunned their town. And though his heart is closed, Jones's sense of duty isn't letting anyone hurt what is his.

#2084 CANYON CRIME SCENE
The Lost Girls • by Carol Ericson
Cade Larson needs LAPD fingerprint expert Lori Del Valle's help tracking down his troubled sister. And when fingerprints link Cade's sister to another missing woman—and a potentially nefarious treatment center—Lori volunteers to go undercover. Will their dangerous plan bring a predator to justice or tragically end their reunion?

YOU CAN FIND MORE INFORMATION ON UPCOMING HARLEQUIN TITLES, FREE EXCERPTS AND MORE AT HARLEQUIN.COM.

HICNM0522

"CHELSEA, WHAT'S GOING ON?" Johnny clutched his cell
phone to his ear and at the same time he sat up and turned
on the lamp on his nightstand.

"That man...that man is here. He tried to b-break in."
The words came amid sobs. "He...he was at my back
d-door and breaking the gl-glass to get in."

"Hang up and call Lane," he instructed as he got out
of bed.

"I...already called, but n-nobody is here yet."

Johnny could hear the abject terror in her voice, and an
icy fear shot through him. "Where are you now?"

HIEXP0522

"I'm in the kitchen."

"Get to the bathroom and lock yourself in. Do you hear me? Lock yourself in the bathroom, and I'll be there as quickly as I can," he instructed.

"Please hurry. I don't know where he is now, and I'm so scared."

"Just get to the bathroom. Lock the door and don't open it for anyone but me or the police." He hung up and quickly dressed. He then strapped on his gun and left his cabin. Any residual sleepiness he might have felt was instantly gone, replaced by a sharp edge of tension that tightened his chest.

Don't miss
Closing in on the Cowboy *by Carla Cassidy,*
available July 2022 wherever
Harlequin Intrigue books and ebooks are sold.

Harlequin.com

HARLEQUIN

Heartfelt or thrilling, passionate or uplifting—Harlequin is more than just happily-ever-after.

With twelve different series to choose from and new books available every month, you are sure to find stories that will move you, uplift you, inspire and delight you.

SIGN UP FOR THE HARLEQUIN NEWSLETTER

Be the first to hear about great new reads and exciting offers!

Harlequin.com/newsletters

Love Harlequin romance?

DISCOVER.

Be the first to find out about promotions,
news and exclusive content!

Facebook.com/HarlequinBooks

Twitter.com/HarlequinBooks

Instagram.com/HarlequinBooks

Pinterest.com/HarlequinBooks

YouTube.com/HarlequinBooks

ReaderService.com

EXPLORE.

Sign up for the Harlequin e-newsletter and
download a free book from any series at
TryHarlequin.com

CONNECT.

Join our Harlequin community to
share your thoughts and connect
with other romance readers!
Facebook.com/groups/HarlequinConnection